LAW...

Big E... ...
travel... ...guns and is ready
to use them both.

Emmitt Hawthorne: The prosperous rancher has left behind a fortune in cattle and land—and a bitter struggle between his two very different sons.

Malcolm Hawthorne: The natural choice to take over the Boxed H Ranch, the hardworking elder son of Emmitt Hawthorne has a will to back up his claim. Or is it an elaborate fake?

Scott Hawthorne: Emmitt's handsome, reckless younger son would rather be reining in women than roping steers. But when he wants to he can turn serious. Deadly serious.

Lorna Hawthorne: Emmitt's daughter has lived a sheltered life on the Boxed H Ranch. Now a local businessman is promising her marriage, and her brothers are fighting to the death.

Jessica Prentice: She is one of the rarest things in the West—a woman lawyer. She's won over the men in her profession, and a judge named Earl Stark.

Cahoon: He is a gun for hire who has always managed to keep one foot inside the law. In the Hawthorne dispute, he meets a man as ruthless as he is.

PRAISE FOR JAMES M. REASONER'S *STARK'S JUSTICE*

"A great beginning for a rousing new series by one of the best writers. Big Earl Stark has the Western savvy of the Sacketts and the courtroom cunning of Perry Mason. I can't wait to read his next exploit!"
—Bill Crider, author of *Ryan Rides Back* and *Galveston Gunman*

Books by James M. Reasoner

Stark's Justice
The Hawthorne Legacy

Published by Pocket Books

For orders other than by individual consumers, Pocket Books grants a discount on the purchase of **10 or more** copies of single titles for special markets or premium use. For further details, please write to the Vice-President of Special Markets, Pocket Books, 1230 Avenue of the Americas, New York, NY 10020.

For information on how individual consumers can place orders, please write to Mail Order Department, Paramount Publishing, 200 Old Tappan Road, Old Tappan, NJ 07675.

A JUDGE EARL STARK WESTERN
JAMES M. REASONER

THE HAWTHORNE LEGACY

 Producers of **The First Americans, The White Indian,** and **The Holts.**

Book Creations Inc., Canaan, NY • Lyle Kenyon Engel, Founder

POCKET BOOKS
New York   London   Toronto   Sydney   Tokyo   Singapore

The sale of this book without its cover is unauthorized. If you purchased this book without a cover, you should be aware that it was reported to the publisher as "unsold and destroyed." Neither the author nor the publisher has received payment for the sale of this "stripped book."

This book is a work of fiction. Names, characters, places and incidents are products of the author's imagination or are used fictitiously. Any resemblance to actual events or locales or persons, living or dead, is entirely coincidental.

An *Original* Publication of POCKET BOOKS

POCKET BOOKS, a division of Simon & Schuster Inc.
1230 Avenue of the Americas, New York, NY 10020

Copyright © 1994 by Book Creations Inc.

All rights reserved, including the right to reproduce this book or portions thereof in any form whatsoever. For information address Pocket Books, 1230 Avenue of the Americas, New York, NY 10020

ISBN: 0-671-87141-2

First Pocket Books printing June 1994

10 9 8 7 6 5 4 3 2 1

POCKET and colophon are registered trademarks of Simon & Schuster Inc.

Cover art by Darryl Zudeck

Printed in the U.S.A.

This book is dedicated to the memory of Leonard F. Meares, a fine writer and a consummate professional, but most of all a good friend who left us too soon.

THE HAWTHORNE LEGACY

Prologue

". . . and as I look out upon you this afternoon, I am reminded that each man has his own story to tell in this life, that the features we present to the world may not delineate the entirety of our beings. In other words, things are not always as they seem, young gentlemen. The task will fall to you as attorneys-at-law to cut through all the obfuscation and deception, to peer through the haze of confusion and falsity, to discover the clear and shining beacon of Truth!

"Truth, of course, being a relative matter . . .

"At this point, I feel that I must depart from my prepared remarks, because I can tell from the expressions on the faces of some that not all of you fully comprehend what I am saying. Perhaps I can illustrate my point with a slight reminiscence, a story of the days when I first sat on the bench in this great and glorious

West of ours. If you will permit me to move out from behind this podium . . . A good trial lawyer uses every weapon at his disposal, gentlemen, and those weapons include his very presence, the way he conducts himself, the excitement that grips him as he slashes aside all the barriers that obscure the true facts of the case. . . . There, that's better.

"Now, as I was saying—and I pray you will pardon my pacing back and forth, an old habit I learned in front of juries that were sometimes hostile to my clients—as I was saying, things are not always as they seem. Take, for example, the case of a man named Emmitt Hawthorne and the disposal of his estate—a vast estate, I might add—following his untimely death. It all began in the far western reaches of the great state of Texas, on a winding road between the frontier communities of Harker's Crossing and Delgado. . . ."

—Excerpt from the commencement address
delivered by Judge Earl Stark
to the Law School Class of 1895,
Western States College

Chapter One

> "'Ol' Sally she was beautiful
> with skin as soft as beaver hide!
> I would'a married that sweet gal
> if Sally hadn't up and died!'"

Barney McCullum and Ace-High Ashton swayed in their saddles and bellowed out the maudlin words of the song as they rode along the trail between Harker's Crossing and Delgado, Texas. It was early morning, not long after sunup, and they'd had themselves a fine old time the night before in Delgado, guzzling rotgut at the Red Horse Saloon, bucking the tiger at the faro tables, and finally picking out a couple of fine-looking *nymphes de la prairie* to take upstairs for a little slap-and-tickle. As it turned out, Barney and Ace-High were so drunk that slapping and tickling was about all they could manage, but the girls told them how wonderful and manly they were, and that was enough for them. They staggered out of the Red Horse as the sun was peeking over the horizon, with a glow about them almost as bright as that fiery orb. They were drunk as skunks and mighty pleased with themselves.

Neither one gave a single thought to what was going to happen to them when they got back to the Double W Bar.

By now, though, something was beginning to stir in the back of Barney's brain, and as Ace-High launched into another song, this one a bawdy ballad concerning a sheepherder's daughter and three poor cowboys, Barney hiccuped a couple of times and frowned. The whiskey was finally wearing off, and visions of the future were taking shape. The images weren't crystal clear yet, but they were clear enough for Barney to make out what he and his pard would be facing when they got back to the ranch.

Barney lifted one hand to his temple, which was starting to throb, and said fervently, "Shut up, Ace!"

Ace-High blinked in surprise and fell silent, glaring blearily at his partner. After a moment he asked, "What bug got up your butt?"

"It ain't a bug I'm worried about. But Winthrop's liable to chew our butts right off when we come draggin' in. We wasn't supposed to stay in town last night, and you know it."

Ace-High shrugged, a gesture that threw off his delicate balance and nearly made him fall out of the saddle. He grabbed the horn and hung on tightly, pulling himself upright again. "If Mr. High-and-Mighty Wade Winthrop lights into us," he said, "hell, we'll just draw our time and ride away. We been wantin' to head up toward the Panhandle, anyway."

"Ride away on what?" asked Barney. "These are Double W Bar horses, or had you forgot about that? We ain't had our own nags since that poker game over at Harker's Crossin' last month."

"Oh, yeah," Ace-High mused. If only he had lived up to his nickname during that game, he would still have his own horse. It was a bitter memory, and it sobered him up a little.

"All right," Barney said. "What we got to do is take whatever Mr. Winthrop dishes out. Won't be the first time we been yelled at."

"Nor probably the last," Ace-High put in.

"Reckon you're right about that. But that's the lot that falls to the likes of us. We cowpokes do the work that keeps this whole blasted country goin', but nobody understands when we got to blow off a little steam—"

Barney stopped abruptly. He could have gone on feeling sorry for himself until he was as blue as the wide Texas sky, but instead he pulled his horse to a halt and stood up in the stirrups, peering down the trail.

"Something's wrong with the bridge," he muttered.

"The hell you say!" Ace-High squinted into the distance, looking in the same direction as his partner. "The bridge over Espantosa Gorge?"

"Ain't no other bridges around here, are there?" Barney asked disgustedly. "Looks like part of it's fallen down."

"Aw, no! How'n hell we gonna get home?"

"Ride around, I reckon. There's a crossing upstream."

"Yeah, fifteen miles upstream!" Ace-High rubbed a shaky hand over his face. "We'll be doin' good to get back to the Double W Bar by noon."

Barney heeled his mount into motion again. "Come on," he said over his shoulder. "I want to take a closer look at that bridge."

Ace-High hesitated only a second, then followed. He usually did what Barney suggested, since Barney was a hell of a lot smarter than he. At least that was what Barney claimed.

The country through which they were riding was semiarid desert dotted with mesquite trees. This was cattle country—it wasn't good for much of anything else—and the vegetation was so sparse that only a huge spread could support a herd large enough to be profitable. There were several such ranches in the low rolling hills north and west of Delgado and Harker's Crossing, among them Wade Winthrop's Double W Bar and old Emmitt Hawthorne's Boxed H.

Running north and south across the rugged landscape in front of Barney and Ace-High was the Espantosa River, which over the centuries had carved a deep gorge into the earth. The gorge was only about fifty feet wide, but it was all of three hundred feet deep; its rocky sides plunged in a sheer drop to a sparkling ribbon of water at the bottom. The gorge was forty miles long. The road crossed it some fifteen miles south of where it began, and the bridge was a veritable lifeline to the ranches in the area. Delgado was closer than Harker's Crossing to nearly all the cattlemen and other settlers, so that was where they did their shopping and business, but it was situated on the far side of Espantosa Gorge from most of them. If anything happened to the bridge, folks could still go into Harker's Crossing, but it would be damned inconvenient for many.

Not to mention inconvenient right now for a couple of rannies like him and Ace-High, Barney thought as they rode toward the bridge. Now that they were closer, he could see that the damage was worse than he had thought. The high wooden railing and the support beams on the south side of the bridge were completely gone. The floor of the bridge sagged toward the gap at a dizzying angle.

"Damn!" Ace-High exclaimed as he and Barney reined in on the little knoll overlooking the east end of the span. "There's no way we can get across that!"

"It'd be suicide to try, plain and simple," Barney agreed. He crossed his hands on the saddlehorn and leaned forward to study the situation. He knew the Espantosa was running a little higher than usual right now because of heavy rains the week before in the hills to the north, and he wondered if a log or some other debris had come floating downstream and collided with one of the supports, knocking it loose. If that was what had happened, the weight of the bridge itself would have caused the whole thing to buckle in a hurry.

What if there had been somebody on the bridge when it happened? Barney suddenly wondered.

His spine tingled at the thought. If somebody had been on the bridge when it started to collapse, he might have been able to get clear, but that would have been cutting it close. Perhaps a good horse that kept its head could have managed to work its way to the other end.

But a moment's hesitation would be fatal.

Barney nudged his horse to a walk, heading slowly down the knoll toward the brink of the gorge. Behind him, Ace-High demanded, "What'n hell are you doin', Barney? Be careful, blast it!"

"I want to take a look down there, make sure nobody got caught on the bridge when it fell down."

"What business is that of our'n?"

"None," Barney admitted. "But I'm curious. I got a bad feelin' about this, Ace."

"I got a bad feelin', too," Ace-High groused, "but I think most of it's from that whiskey we drank last night. I want to go home."

"Go on, then. I'll catch up to you."

Ace-High grimaced and took off his battered Stetson to scratch his head. Barney was getting mighty close to the edge of the gorge now, and Ace-High didn't want him falling into that damned hole in the ground. They had been riding together for nearly five years now, and Barney was as good a pard as a man could want.

"Oh, hell," Ace-High said abruptly. "Hang on, Barney, I'll come with you."

Barney's horse shied nervously as it drew closer to the rim. "All right, all right," Barney muttered to the animal as he reined in again and swung down from the saddle. Caliche dust rose in puffs around his boots when his feet hit the surface of the road. He dropped the reins and approached the drop-off, taking it slow and easy.

The ruined bridge was to his right as he leaned forward to peer down into the gorge. He knew the sides of the cut were not completely smooth—there were a few narrow ledges, although it was difficult to see them from up here—but it would be next to impossible for a man tumbling over that rim to find anything to grab on to.

Something caught his eye, a splash of color on the sandstone about halfway down the wall beneath him, at a place where the wall bulged out a little. It was a big scratch, as if something had slammed into the soft rock and glanced off. The bad feeling in Barney's stomach grew stronger. He heard Ace-High come up beside him, and a second later the other cowboy said, "See, ain't nothin' down there. Now let's head back to the ranch—"

"Wait," Barney said. "Look yonder." He pointed downstream from the bridge. The river was flowing briskly in its channel, a couple of feet higher than normal, but it hadn't quite reached the rock shelf jutting out from the shore.

"Oh, my Lord," Ace-High breathed. "Is that what it looks like?"

"A horse," Barney agreed. "Or what's left of one after it hit that rock. And look, there's something else scattered around it."

Ace-High's curiosity got the best of him, and he leaned out even farther. "What is that?"

"Looks like a carriage that's been busted all to pieces. That horse ain't got a saddle on it, so I reckon it was pullin' that carriage across when the bridge went. The driver must've whipped it up and tried to get off in time but didn't quite make it. You can see where the carriage bounced off the wall down there, then fell the rest of the way."

"Son of a bitch," Ace-High said solemnly. "Then whoever was drivin' that rig . . ." He left the rest of the gruesome thought unsaid.

Barney drew a deep breath. "I reckon the poor fella must've gone into the river and washed on down toward the Rio Grande." He straightened from his crouch. "Come on. We got to go back to Delgado."

"Back to Delgado? But what about Mr. Winthrop?"

"He'll understand when we tell him we had to warn folks in town about the Espantosa bridge bein' out. Besides, we got to find Sheriff Brewster and let him know about that rig down there."

Ace-High scrubbed a hand over his stubbled chin. "Reckon you're right. It's our, what you call it, civic duty, huh?"

"Yeah." Barney strode back to his horse and stepped up into the saddle, Ace-High doing likewise. They turned their mounts around and pointed them east, toward the settlement five miles away. Both cowboys were stone-cold sober now, their drunken hilarity shocked out of them by the grisly discovery they had just made.

As he rode, Barney wondered who the unfortunate soul was who had gone off the bridge and into the river. Unless the carriage provided some clues, folks might never know. The body was probably a long way downstream by now and might not stop until it reached the Rio Grande. It was even possible the corpse would wind up in the Gulf of Mexico, food for the sharks. Barney had been to the Gulf once, to Corpus Christi, and as he was looking out over the blue water the thought had occurred to him that thousands, maybe even millions of creatures were out there, gliding unseen under the surface, hungry and waiting for some poor cowboy foolish enough to go wading into the surf.

Right after that, he had gotten back on his horse and headed for West Texas again.

Sure, all sorts of predators and scavengers were out here, too, like coyotes and rattlers and scorpions and buzzards, but at least a man could *see* the blamed varmints most of the time. It wasn't like the sea, where all the dangers were hidden.

Barney shook his head. He didn't know where the hell all those thoughts had come from; he was hundreds of miles from the ocean and not likely to go there ever again. But he hoped for the sake of the dead man that the poor gent didn't wind up floating out to sea.

He shuddered and heeled his horse into a run. Ace-High did his best to keep up.

Chapter Two

Sheriff Phil Brewster leaned back in the chair behind his desk and propped his booted feet on the drawer he had pulled out. Some men would have put their feet on the desktop, but Brewster had always thought that made him look lazy. He was a mite deliberate at times, but not lazy, and he didn't want any of the citizens of Delgado to get the wrong idea. Brewster wasn't an overly proud man, but he wanted the townspeople to take him seriously. After all, he was the law in these parts.

When he was comfortable, the sheriff busied himself filling his pipe from a beaded tobacco pouch, then struck a kitchen match and lit it. He exhaled, his drooping gray mustache fluttering as he did so. Clouds of foul-smelling smoke wreathed his head. He was content.

The Hawthorne Legacy

That was when two wild-eyed cowboys came bursting into the office, yelling about somebody being dead at the bottom of Espantosa Gorge.

Brewster sat up straight and put his pipe on the desk. "Hold on, damn it," he barked as he rose to his full height. He rested his bony knuckles on the scarred desktop and went on, "I can't make head nor tail of what you boys are sayin'. Start over, and this time just one of you tell it."

Each cowboy took a deep breath and started to speak again. Brewster held up his hands and said, "Shut up!" He pointed to the man on his right. "You. You tell it."

The cowboy, who looked like a typical forty-a-month-and-found line rider, gulped down more air and said, "My name's Barney McCullum, Sheriff, and this here is Ace-High Ashton. We ride for the Double W Bar."

Brewster nodded. "Reckon I recognize the two of you now. You were over at the Red Horse last night when I was makin' my rounds, weren't you?"

McCullum nodded. "That's right. In fact, we was there all night and started back out to Mr. Winthrop's spread about sunup."

"Wade Winthrop ain't likely to be too happy about that. He likes to have his hands ready for a day's work when the rooster crows." Brewster looked out the window and saw that the morning was well advanced. "You boys've lost nearly half a day already."

"Tell us about it," muttered the one called Ace-High, but McCullum shushed him and went on.

"We was ridin' up to the Espantosa bridge when we noticed something was wrong about it," the cowboy said. "The railin' and the support beams on the south side had all collapsed."

Brewster stiffened, a frown appearing on his leathery face. "Collapsed? The whole bridge is down?"

McCullum shook his head. "Not the whole bridge, but enough of it so that nobody could get over it. I reckon the whole shootin' match might go if there was very much weight put on it."

"Well, that's a good thing to know," Brewster said. "Could be dangerous, though I don't see how anybody could start over the bridge and not notice there was something wrong with it. I'll ride out there and post a warnin' sign and wire the sheriff over in Harker's Crossing to do the same on his side."

"That ain't the worst of it, Sheriff," McCullum said. He licked his lips nervously. "I don't reckon anybody would fall in there by mistake, but I'm afraid somebody was on the bridge when it collapsed."

"The hell you say!" Brewster burst out. "Did you see 'em?"

Both cowboys were quick to shake their heads. "All we saw was a dead horse and what was left of a carriage, down there on that shelf right beside the river," McCullum told the lawman. "There weren't no sign of whoever was drivin' the rig, or any passengers it might've been carryin'."

Brewster shook his head. This was a tragedy, a sure enough tragedy. "I'll round up some men and ride out there right away," he muttered. "Liable to need some help findin' out what happened and recoverin' any poor bastard who's still down there in the gorge. You boys are comin' along."

The Hawthorne Legacy

"We really got to get back to the Double W Bar—" Ace-High began.

"I'll take care of Winthrop," Brewster snapped. "I'll officially deputize the two of you if that'll help. Raise your right hands."

Barney and Ace-High swallowed hard and looked as if they wished they were somewhere else, but they did as Brewster said and hastily stumbled through the oath he told them to repeat. Then he sent them out to round up at least half a dozen more volunteers for the trip to Espantosa Gorge.

Once the two cowboys were gone, Brewster sighed heavily. He had a vague idea of who might have been driving that carriage when it fell into the gorge, but he hoped he was wrong. He hated to wish such a grim fate on any innocent travelers, but it would be better if the poor, doomed son of a bitch had been a stranger just passing through.

Brewster basically liked peace and quiet, and if his hunch was right, all hell was liable to start popping around here.

The thing to do was not to jump to any conclusions. Phil Brewster told himself that all the way out to the gorge as he rode at the head of the makeshift rescue party. He was calling it a rescue party even though there wasn't a chance in hell anyone was still alive at the bottom of that gorge to rescue. Not after a drop of three hundred feet. The only questions were whether or not they could find the body, or bodies, and identify them.

It was enough to make a man wish he hadn't eaten

such a big breakfast. His wife's flapjacks and bacon and scrambled eggs were sitting at the bottom of Brewster's gullet, making him feel as if he had swallowed one of those twelve-pound cannonballs that sat next to the old, rusted, plugged-up Confederate cannons on the courthouse lawn.

Not everybody was so leery of what the rescue party would find at Espantosa Gorge. In fact, the mood of the group was almost cheery. Nothing too dramatic happened in Delgado these days. The Comanches were all settled down and had been for quite a while, and the Apaches who still raided now and then in the Big Bend never came up this far. Occasionally some cowboys would get too liquored up, imagine themselves to be desperadoes, then stop a stagecoach and hold up the passengers. But that was about as lawless as it ever got around Delgado. And that was the way Brewster liked it.

Of course, a bridge collapsing wasn't the same as an Indian attack or a stage holdup, but that hadn't stopped over a dozen townsmen from volunteering to accompany the sheriff and his two "deputies." The riders behind Brewster were buzzing with conversation. They sounded almost anxious to reach the gorge and peer down at the death and destruction.

Maybe he was getting old, Brewster thought, but he saw nothing particularly exciting or thrilling about a tragedy. Especially a tragedy like this one that could have far-reaching effects . . .

But he didn't know yet who had been driving that carriage, he reminded himself. It was best not to get carried away so soon.

The Hawthorne Legacy

A little over an hour after leaving Delgado, the riders reached the gorge, and Brewster motioned them to a halt on the knoll overlooking what was left of the bridge. "Dismount here," he told them. "We'll go the rest of the way on foot. Don't want anybody's horse getting spooked."

That took some of the jolliness out of their mood, Brewster noted. He handed the reins of his horse to Ace-High Ashton, who volunteered to stay there and tend to everyone's animals. "I've already seen what's down there," Ace-High said with a shudder. "Don't need to see it again."

Brewster didn't argue with him; somebody had to stay behind and hold the horses. He hitched up his belt and told the posse, "Come on, fellas, but watch your step. We don't want no more accidents."

Faced with the gorge itself, the townies settled down right away. It was one thing to talk excitedly about a bridge collapsing but another thing entirely to stare down into three hundred feet of nothingness. Brewster felt a little weak-kneed himself as he approached the rim.

When he leaned out and looked down, he saw the dead horse. It was hard to miss. He grunted in distaste at the sight and looked away, then forced himself to look again. Just as McCullum and Ashton had said, the wreckage of what appeared to be an utterly destroyed carriage was scattered around the horse and along the ledge of rock that overhung the water.

"I don't see anybody, only the horse," one of the men said. "You think the body washed downstream, Sheriff?"

"Likely," Brewster said. "I'll be needin' volunteers to go down there with me and make sure, though."

The townies looked at him in surprise. "Down there?" one of them croaked.

Brewster nodded. "It can be done. Folks have climbed into and out of this gorge plenty of times in the past. Done it myself, in fact, in my younger days. There ain't been no need the past fifteen years, since the bridge was built." He pointed out a faint line that seemed to waver down the near wall of the gorge. "See that? It's a trail, sort of. There's places the ledge ain't more than a foot wide, but it's easier than that most of the way. As long as a man's careful, he can make it with no trouble. Same way on the other side."

Barney McCullum spoke up. "I'll go with you, Sheriff. Sort of my responsibility, seein' as it was me and Ace-High who found the bridge this way."

"I ain't orderin' you to, McCullum. Anybody who climbs down with me has got to be willin'."

Two of the men from Delgado stepped forward, both of them young and anxious not to be shown up by a cowhand. Brewster nodded and said, "The rest of you fellas get your ropes from your saddles and start knottin' 'em together. We'll rig a sort of safety line so we'll have something to hang on to when we start down."

When the ropes were tied together, one end was tossed into the gorge and the other dallied around a couple of mesquites and then tied to one of the heavy posts that anchored the bridge on the east end. With Brewster going first, the four men grasped the rope and started the nerve-racking descent. As he carefully placed his boots on the narrow ledge, Brewster remembered the old saying that it wasn't the fall that killed a man—it was the landing.

Somehow that didn't make him feel any better.

It took over an hour of careful climbing to reach the bottom of the gorge, and Brewster's shirt was soaked with sweat when he got there. His heart was pounding heavily. He could tell the other men weren't in any better shape. As he stepped out onto the wide stone shelf where the carriage had landed and felt solid ground under his feet again, he drew a deep breath of relief, trying not to think about the fact that they would still have to climb back out of the gorge.

The air was cooler here than up above; although there was little breeze in the gorge, the high walls of the cut kept it in perpetual shadow. Upstream, the Espantosa went through a series of rapids. The roaring was audible here, and there was a faint, cool mist in the air.

"Take a good look around," Brewster said to the other men, raising his voice to be heard over the sound of the rapids. "See if there's anybody behind those rocks." He pointed to some jagged boulders along the base of the wall.

The sheriff walked to the edge of the shelf and knelt to peer into the water. A body could have been snagged by a submerged rock or log, he thought. The river was a little murky because of the runoff from the hills, but it was still clear enough for him to see that nothing was under the surface, at least right here. The shelf ran about a hundred yards downstream before petering out, and he followed it the whole way, his keen eyes searching the rapid current for any sign of a body.

McCullum came over to him. "We didn't find a thing, Sheriff," he reported. "I reckon whoever was on that carriage is long gone by now, headed on down to the gulf." A little shudder ran through him as he spoke.

"Maybe so," Brewster said. He pulled his mustache for a second and then, his face set in a taut mask, walked over to the dead horse and the wrecked carriage.

He saw three wheels but not the fourth and figured it must have gone into the river. Much of the carriage was smashed into kindling, but a few larger pieces, still intact, were scattered about. He picked one up and examined it. The vehicle had been painted black, like a hearse. That was a bad sign; Brewster knew a man who drove a black carriage. He tossed the chunk of wood down and looked around for another piece, something that might confirm his hunch.

McCullum found it first. He said, "Look here, Sheriff," and thrust a good-sized section of wreckage toward Brewster.

The lawman recognized it as what was left of a door. He recognized, too, the symbol painted on the outside in gold leaf, plainly visible against the black background even though it had been chipped and scratched in the fall. The emblem was a simple one—nothing gaudy or fancy about it—like the man it belonged to. It was a capital letter *H* with a square around it.

Boxed H. Emmitt Hawthorne's brand.

McCullum began, "Don't that belong to—"

"I know who it belongs to," Brewster said sharply. "Come on, boys, we might as well climb out of here."

"Are we going back to town?" one of the men asked.

"You can if you want to." Brewster looked up at the

sky, a narrow blue band high above them. "I got something else to do."

He had to pay a visit to Hawthorne's ranch, had to find out who had been driving that carriage and how bad a catastrophe this really was. But he was already sure of one thing.

No matter what he found at the Boxed H, life around Delgado was never going to be the same again.

Chapter Three

It was midafternoon before Sheriff Brewster, Barney McCullum, Ace-High Ashton, and several of the other men from Delgado arrived at the Boxed H ranch. The other members of the party had gone back to the settlement while Brewster and his companions took the long way around to Emmitt Hawthorne's cattle spread. The ranch was vast, hundreds of square miles of Texas plains. Its headquarters sat smack-dab in the middle.

Brewster had known Emmitt Hawthorne for over twenty years, and Hawthorne had been an old-timer in this part of the country when Brewster first arrived. Hawthorne had crossed the Pecos as a young man, striking out across what was then an untamed wilderness that only a few white men had seen. He had found the place he wanted to settle and had held the land ever since against Indians, rustlers, drought in the summer, and blizzards in the winter. He had cut down timber in the mountains to the north and hauled it back by wagon. He had built a house, a huge, rambling, three-story affair of logs, adobe, and whitewashed planks. The mansion had a crazy-quilt look to it and might have appeared to some to be the creation of a madman, but Brewster had visited there many times and had to admit the place had a certain bizarre charm to it.

Hawthorne had built the house for his wife, a gentle southern belle from East Texas named Lila, and when he was finished, he sent for her. By that time he had a crew of over forty hands, a mix of Mexican *vaqueros* and wild young Texas cowboys, and a herd of more than a thousand longhorns. The herd grew steadily, as did the Boxed H crew. And once Lila had arrived, so in time did the Hawthorne family.

A year after she came to the Boxed H, Malcolm Hawthorne was born, followed two years later by his brother, Scott. The next two Hawthorne children did not survive infancy, Brewster recalled; one, a little girl, had been stung by a scorpion, and the other, a boy, had fallen victim to a fever. Finally, Lorna, the baby of the family, had been born, a beautiful tow-headed child who had grown up as something of a tomboy and was now turning into a lovely young woman.

Unfortunately, Lila Hawthorne had not lived to see that. Cholera had claimed her four, no, nearly five years earlier, Brewster remembered. He had been a pallbearer at her funeral, when she was laid to rest in the family burial ground on a hill overlooking the ranch house. Lila and the two ill-fated children were the only ones buried there, although Emmitt had always said that he would rest beside them someday.

If Emmitt had been at the reins of that carriage, he'd never have the chance to lie down for eternity beside his beloved Lila, the sheriff thought grimly as he rode past the cemetery and down the hill toward the ranch house.

No one came out to meet the riders as they approached, and that was a bad sign in itself. The dogs were barking, heralding the arrival of strangers, and if Emmitt had been at home, he would have stepped out onto the long porch to see who was coming. Brewster glanced toward the barns and corrals and saw a few cowboys moving around, but there was no sign of the small, brisk figure of the ranch's owner. Emmitt was not an impressive-looking man—he was slender and a bit below medium height—but once you got to know him, you realized just how tough he was. Brewster had never seen him unshaven, and when he wasn't working on horseback, he always wore a plain black suit and a neatly knotted string tie, looking as much like a businessman as the cattle baron he really was. Age had finally started to catch up to him in recent years, and he had taken to riding around in that black carriage, handling the reins himself, rather than galloping all over the Boxed H on a saddle horse, as he had in earlier times.

Brewster reined up in front of the house, and as he did someone finally came out onto the porch to see what all the commotion was about. Lorna Hawthorne smiled up at the sheriff. She was twenty years old, but she still had the coltish figure of a girl. Her blond hair fell in lush waves past her shoulders. She wore a man's shirt with the sleeves rolled up, denim pants, and boots, but there was an apron tied over the outfit. Lorna had taken over the running of the household after her mother's death, and that responsibility for the feminine chores was always at war with her desire to be out on horseback, helping with the roping and branding.

"Hello, Sheriff," she called brightly. "What brings you out here?".

Brewster tried not to look too grim and worried as he said, "I'm lookin' for your daddy, Miss Lorna. Would he be around?"

She shook her head. "I'm afraid not. You might've caught him in town. He started for Delgado early this morning."

The sheriff's breath hissed between his clenched teeth. He had been hoping against hope that someone else was driving Emmitt Hawthorne's carriage when it fell off that bridge. He knew he shouldn't wish such a fate on either of the Hawthorne boys or on one of the ranch hands, but he hadn't been able to suppress the thought.

"I suppose he was drivin' that carriage of his?"

"That's right," Lorna said. She was beginning to frown a little. "Is something wrong, Sheriff?"

"I'm afraid so. Mind if we get down?"

"Of course not." Lorna motioned for the visitors to dismount. She looked worried as she went on, "Something bad has happened, hasn't it?"

Brewster put off answering the question by asking one of his own. "Are your brothers around the house, Miss Lorna? I'd rather talk to all three of you at the same time."

"Scott's inside and Mal's down at the corrals." Lorna had gone pale beneath her tan. "I'll fetch Scott."

Brewster turned to Barney and Ace-High. "You know Malcolm Hawthorne?"

"Seen him around town," Barney replied.

"Go down to the corrals and find him. Tell him I want to see him."

"Sure, Sheriff." The two cowboys hurried off, looking uncomfortable because they knew why they were running this errand.

Lorna had turned and gone into the house, the screen door banging behind her. Brewster stepped up onto the porch and stood there, turning his hat over awkwardly in his hands. A few minutes went by, and then the door was pushed open again. Scott Hawthorne strode onto the porch, followed by his sister, and demanded, "What the hell is this all about, Sheriff?"

Brewster swallowed his annoyance at Scott's imperious tone. He had never particularly liked Scott Hawthorne. The young man had blond hair a shade darker than his sister's, and although he was only in his late twenties, there was already a look of dissipation about him, a look that came from too many nights spent at the Red Horse Saloon. Too much whiskey, too much gambling, too many women—that was Scott Hawthorne. Even now, this late in the day, he looked as though he had just gotten out of bed. His cheeks were stubbled and his eyes were red and puffy. He was probably hung over, Brewster decided.

"I want to wait until your brother gets here to explain things, Scott," the sheriff said, trying to keep his own voice civil. Out of respect for his old friend Emmitt, he wasn't going to grab Scott by the shoulders and try to shake some sense into him—although

The Hawthorne Legacy

that was what it was going to take, at the very least, if the boy was ever going to amount to anything, Brewster reflected.

"You can tell me anything you can tell Malcolm," snapped Scott. Lorna stood behind him, looking as if she wanted to tell him to be quiet.

Brewster was saved from an argument by the sight of Malcolm Hawthorne striding quickly toward the house from the corrals, followed by Barney and Ace-High. Scott and Lorna both took after Lila, but Malcolm was a larger version of his father, a well-built young man of thirty with curly brown hair. He wore range clothes and was every bit as dusty as the other ranch hands. Brewster knew that Malcolm served as foreman of the Boxed H and did a good job of it.

He stopped at the bottom of the steps and said, "Howdy, Sheriff. These gents said you wanted to see me."

"You and your brother and sister," Brewster told him. "Step on up here, Mal. I'm afraid I've got bad news."

"It's something about Dad," Lorna said. "I know it is."

Malcolm came onto the porch and asked quietly, "Is that true, Sheriff?"

Brewster nodded. There was no good way to deliver this news, so he just said it straight out. "The bridge over Espantosa Gorge partially collapsed sometime last night or early this morning. Your father's carriage was going across when it happened. We found the horse and the wreck of the carriage at the bottom of the gorge, but there was no sign of Emmitt."

The three Hawthorne children stared at him. Lorna

was blinking, her eyes already filling with tears. Scott looked confused, and a bleak expression was settling over Malcolm's face.

Always the practical one, Malcolm asked bluntly, "Are you saying that our father is dead?"

"We didn't find his body, but there's no way he could have survived a fall like that, Mal. You know that as well as I do."

Lorna shook her head and said, "No," then lifted her hands to her face and started to cry.

Scott stood there looking stunned. Malcolm took a deep breath, shoved his hands in his back pockets, and stared down at the floor.

"I'm sure sorry," Brewster told them. "Your daddy and I were friends for a long time. I hate to bother you with questions at a time like this, but I got to know: Was he alone when he left here?"

Malcolm nodded and looked up, his grief-filled eyes meeting Brewster's gaze squarely. "He was alone. He was going to Delgado to take care of some business, he said."

"What kind of business?" asked Brewster.

"I don't know," Malcolm replied, shaking his head. "He'd been pretty closemouthed lately, like something was bothering him, but we figured he'd take care of it, like he always did."

Brewster felt a faint stirring of suspicion, then dismissed it. Nobody could have killed Emmitt by causing the bridge to collapse; that was just too farfetched a notion. Anyway, Emmitt Hawthorne hadn't had any enemies who would do a thing like that. He had stepped on a few toes in his time, more than likely; nobody built up a cattle empire the size of the Boxed

H without rubbing some folks the wrong way. But he had gotten along well with his neighbors, especially Wade Winthrop, who owned the biggest spread in the area other than the Boxed H.

"You feel up to ridin' over to the gorge with us, Mal?" Brewster asked. "Just so's you can identify what's left of the carriage, official-like?"

Before Malcolm could answer, Scott said harshly, "I'll go. I've got just as much right."

"It's not a matter of right," Malcolm told his brother, not bothering to conceal his own ill feeling. "Somebody ought to stay here with Lorna."

She was still crying, but she wiped away some of the tears and declared, "We'll all go. We owe it to Dad."

Neither of her brothers looked comfortable with that decision, and neither was Brewster. He didn't want Lorna to see the horse's carcass spread out over the ledge. But it was no use arguing with her, he knew. She could be as stubborn as an old plow mule when she wanted to, and Brewster could tell by her expression that this was one of those times.

They were all mounted up in short order and heading back toward the gorge. Malcolm, Scott, and Lorna were silent as they rode, lost in their own thoughts. Brewster hoped this tragedy might draw Malcolm and Scott a little closer. He knew there had been friction between them ever since they were little, the sort of antagonism that most brothers eventually grew out of. That hadn't happened with the Hawthorne boys, though. Brewster recalled that Emmitt had often said something about not knowing what would happen once he was gone and no longer able to keep his sons from each other's throats.

Looked like they were all going to find out, the sheriff mused grimly. Maybe Lorna, who got along with everybody, could keep them in line.

They rode straight to the gorge, rather than to the crossing upstream, and reined in on the western edge. The wreckage on the shelf at the bottom could be seen even more plainly from this side. Malcolm leaned forward in the saddle and stared at it for a long moment, then heaved a sigh.

"It's Dad's carriage, all right," he said. "And that's the big bay that was pulling it."

Lorna had only glanced at the dead horse and the debris, then looked away with a sharp intake of breath. Scott was frowning darkly. He looked at the bridge and said, "What the hell happened?"

"No way of knowing for sure," Brewster said. "Something made the supports on the south side give way, and the bridge buckled when they went. Something floatin' downstream from the hills could've smashed into one of the posts and started the whole thing."

"The bridge should have been sturdier, damn it," Scott said. "It shouldn't have fallen down that easily!"

"It's stood up to floods for fifteen years," Brewster pointed out. "I reckon this was a stroke of mighty bad luck."

Lorna said, "You . . . you didn't find Dad's body?"

Brewster shook his head. "No, ma'am. But I'm goin' to send some men downstream, all the way to the end of the gorge. No way of knowin' if they'll find him or not, but we'll sure give it a try."

"But he'll still be dead, even if you do find him,"

Scott said bitterly. He wheeled his horse around without another word and galloped off toward the Boxed H.

Looking older than his years now, Malcolm extended a hand to Brewster and said, "We'll be getting back to the ranch, too, Sheriff. There'll be a lot of things to take care of. Thank you for coming to get us."

Brewster shook hands with the young man. "You know I'd give anything for this not to have happened, Mal. Your daddy was a fine man."

Malcolm nodded, then took Lorna's hand, and side by side they rode away. Brewster watched them, saw the way their shoulders slumped in despair, and his heart went out to them. This was a tragedy that could affect the whole county in the long run, but first and foremost it was a terrible loss for those youngsters.

"Sheriff," Barney McCullum said from beside him, "we ain't goin' to find Mr. Hawthorne's body, are we?"

"Ain't likely," Brewster said as he turned his attention back to the gorge. "But like I told those kids, we got to try. I'd like to see Emmitt Hawthorne laid to rest proper-like in his own ground."

Only it wasn't Emmitt's anymore, Brewster realized, not if Emmitt was dead. The sheriff wondered what was going to happen to the Boxed H now.

Chapter Four

Just as Barney McCullum had predicted, the body of Emmitt Hawthorne was not found. Sheriff Brewster and his men covered both sides of the river and even continued the search for several miles south of where the gorge ended. But the swiftly flowing stream had carried the body away, probably forever.

The Espantosa flowed into the Rio Grande about eighty miles south of Delgado. Brewster wired the authorities down in the border settlements, asking them to notify him if the body of an unidentified man showed up in the river, but he didn't expect anything to come of the effort. There had been enough rain back in the spring so that the Rio was probably running pretty high these days, too.

Like it or not, Emmitt Hawthorne was gone.

The absence of a body didn't mean the old rancher couldn't have a proper send-off, though. In fact, prac-

The Hawthorne Legacy

tically the whole town, as well as ranchers from a hundred miles around, showed up for the memorial service at the Delgado Baptist Church three days after the accident.

As he sat in the first pew with his brother and sister, Malcolm Hawthorne wanted to reach up and rip loose the tie around his neck. He had never liked wearing the blasted things, but Lorna had insisted. She had told him to wear his good suit, too, saying that it would show a lack of respect for their father if Malcolm attended the service in his usual denim pants and work shirt. Malcolm knew she was right, of course, but that didn't make it any more comfortable.

He glanced at Lorna, who was sitting at his right. She was wearing a black dress and veil and quietly weeping as the preacher talked about what a good man Emmitt Hawthorne had been. On Lorna's other side was Scott, who was wearing a dark suit like Malcolm. Unlike his older brother, however, Scott looked perfectly comfortable in the suit. He rarely worked with the stock on the ranch and rarely wore range clothes. He preferred outfits like the one he had on now for riding into town and visiting the Red Horse or one of the other saloons.

Malcolm felt a surge of resentment. Scott had never carried his share of the load on the ranch, leaving it up to his father and brother to see that everything got done. There was no reason to think things were going to change now that Emmitt was gone.

For his part, Scott kept a carefully solemn expression on his face. It wasn't difficult, for he felt genuine sorrow that his father was gone. Emmitt had always thought his younger son didn't respect him, but that wasn't true. Scott could look at what his father had accomplished—forging a ranch like the Boxed H out of nothing but miles of scrub brush and cheat grass and rocks—and feel a great deal of respect. But Scott had never had any desire to follow in Emmitt's footsteps. It had been left to Malcolm to do that, and Scott had never gotten over the fact that Emmitt obviously preferred Malcolm to him.

Emmitt was gone now, and everything was going to be different, Scott thought. For once in their lives, he and Malcolm were on equal footing.

Lorna sat between her brothers and tried not to break down completely. She was still having a difficult time accepting the fact that her father was gone. No, not gone, she corrected herself. *Dead*. To say he was gone implied that he might come back.

But Lorna knew she would never see her father again, at least not this side of heaven.

She turned her head and glanced over her shoulder at the handsome, dark-haired man who sat in the pew directly behind her. He gave her a faint, supportive smile and reached forward to lightly touch her shoulder for a moment. She didn't know what she would have done without Todd Summers. As soon as he had heard about her father's death, he had come out to the Boxed H and taken her into his arms, holding her tightly and telling her that he would do anything he could to help her through this awful time.

Lorna was glad of one thing. She had accepted Todd's proposal of marriage a month earlier, and Emmitt had given the union his blessing. No date had been set, and of course the wedding would have to be put off even longer now, but at least Lorna's father could have the satisfaction of knowing, wherever he was, that his daughter was going to be well taken care of.

Emmitt Hawthorne had no family other than his children, at least not in this area. An older brother had disappeared across the border in Mexico more than thirty years earlier and was probably long dead by now. But Emmitt had had plenty of friends—Sheriff Brewster, Mayor Joseph Pike, Dr. Hardy Silcox, Wade Winthrop, attorney Burton Garrison, merchant Todd Summers, banker Ben Whitehead, the smaller ranchers from the Espantosa basin . . . All of them and many others, including almost the entire crew of the Boxed H, were packed inside the whitewashed walls of the church.

Reverend King launched into a prayer to conclude the memorial service. When he finally said "Amen," Malcolm felt hollow inside as the congregation echoed the benediction. There would be no graveside service, since there was no body to bury, no casket to lower into the earth. He felt almost as if a part of himself were missing as he filed out of the church with the others.

The day was hot. The ladies were fanning themselves, and beads of sweat stood out on the faces of the men. Malcolm and Scott and Lorna shook hands with the other mourners until Malcolm felt his fingers going numb. Todd Summers stood beside Lorna, one hand resting lightly on her left arm. Malcolm was glad the storekeeper was there with her; he himself had never been very good with words, and he wouldn't have known what to say to comfort her.

Finally, when he had stood it as long as he could, Malcolm pulled the tie loose and jerked it from around his neck. "We'd better get back to the ranch," he said. "I want our boys to relieve those riders Mr. Winthrop loaned us to keep an eye on things while we were in town."

"What's the hurry?" Scott asked as he put his black hat on his head. "I thought maybe we'd stop at the Red Horse and get a drink while Todd takes Lorna down to the boardinghouse."

Mrs. Calvin at the boardinghouse had given Lorna a room so that she could rest and change clothes before and after the service.

Malcolm said to his sister, "You go ahead. We'll wait for you." When Lorna and Todd had started down the street and were out of earshot, he turned back to Scott and added in a harsh undertone, "I don't think swilling whiskey is much of a way to show your respect for the dead!"

Scott's lips drew back in a humorless smile. "Name me a better way."

"Taking care of the ranch, for one," Malcolm shot back. "I want those stock in the eastern sections moved up into the hills before the dry weather sets in."

"Mighty quick to start giving orders, aren't you?"

"That's my job, remember?" Malcolm glared at his brother. "I'm the foreman."

"You *were* the foreman," Scott said.

Malcolm's chin lifted defiantly. "What in blazes do you mean by that?" he demanded, still keeping his voice down since they were in front of the church. It was a struggle to hang on to his temper, though.

"Dad picked you to run the ranch, but he's not here anymore. Who's to say who's running things now?"

After a moment it dawned on Malcolm what his brother was getting at, and he asked incredulously, "Surely you don't think *you're* going to take over?"

The Hawthorne Legacy

"Why not? I know as much about running that ranch as you do. Hell, I know more about the business end of things. You never cracked a ledger book in your life."

"I was too busy making sure the cattle were fed and watered and taken care of," Malcolm said hotly, his voice rising. "If you think you're going to waltz in and start giving orders—"

"Hold on there, Mal." The voice came from behind him, accompanied by a firm hand that grasped his shoulder. He turned to see Sheriff Brewster, who was looking at him with some concern. Beside the lawman was the solid, white-bearded form of Burton Garrison, Emmitt's attorney.

Brewster went on, "You boys shouldn't be fightin' out here in front of the church like this, right after your daddy's service. It ain't fittin'."

"The sheriff's right," Garrison said in his deep voice. "Emmitt would have expected better of you lads."

Malcolm grimaced in embarrassment. Brewster and Garrison were right, of course. He respected both of them. Brewster might be a little slow-moving and slow-talking, but he was a dependable lawman and as honest as the day was long. Garrison, originally an easterner, had come west and developed a thriving practice in Delgado, adding clients until he'd had to take in a partner.

"I reckon we can hash this out later," Malcolm said as he looked at Scott, whose features had settled back into their usual sullen mask. "We were just talking about who's going to run things at the ranch now."

"I want to discuss that very subject with you two, and with your sister," Garrison said. "Do you think the three of you could stop by my office before you head back to the Boxed H?"

Malcolm frowned, unsure just what the lawyer might have to say to them, but he nodded. "I'll fetch Lorna from the boardinghouse." He couldn't resist adding to Scott, "I suppose you can find your way over to Mr. Garrison's office from the Red Horse?"

"Don't worry about me," Scott snapped. He turned and started down the street toward the saloon.

Brewster watched him go and said to Malcolm, "I been hopin' you boys'd quit this feudin'."

"Talk to Scott," Malcolm said. "I'm willing to get along anytime he is."

Deep down, though, he had to ask himself if that was true. Scott had always gotten away with things that Malcolm never would have, and Malcolm wondered if that had made him resent Scott to the point that he could *never* feel brotherly toward him. If that was true, it was a damned shame. But one thing was certain—Scott was going to have to meet him halfway if there was to be any sort of truce.

Malcolm walked down the street to the boardinghouse and found Todd Summers waiting in the parlor. "Lorna will be right down," the storekeeper said as he stood up.

Malcolm nodded distractedly, still thinking about the meeting Garrison had requested. He paced back and forth across the room and said, "My father's lawyer wants to see Lorna and Scott and me."

Todd sat down and crossed his legs, holding his bowler hat on his lap. "Must be about your dad's last will and testament," he mused.

Malcolm stopped his pacing and frowned. Will? He

hadn't even thought about a will. Maybe that would settle the argument between Scott and him about who would run the Boxed H from now on.

"Your father *did* have a will, didn't he?" Todd asked.

"You know, I'm not sure. I don't think he ever discussed it with us." Malcolm started pacing again. "But he must have had Mr. Garrison draw one up. It wasn't like Dad not to be prepared for something."

"A lot of people don't like to think about their own deaths," Todd pointed out. "Some of them seem to believe they'll jinx themselves by worrying about things like wills."

Malcolm shook his head. "Dad wasn't that way."

And yet, try as he might, he couldn't remember Emmitt ever saying anything about a will or otherwise indicating how he wanted the three of them to split up their inheritance. Maybe Todd was right. He'd ask Garrison about it, Malcolm decided. The three of them had the right to know as soon as possible.

Lorna came down the stairs a few minutes later, dressed once more in the tan traveling outfit she had worn into town. "I'm ready to go back to the ranch," she said when she saw Malcolm waiting in the parlor.

"We can't leave just yet," he told her. "Mr. Garrison wants to see all three of us at his office."

Lorna frowned and looked at Todd, who shrugged. "I'll be glad to go with you if you want, honey," he told her, "but this is really none of my business."

"No, I suppose not." Lorna sighed and took Malcolm's arm. "Let's get this over with."

They went along the street to the building in which Garrison had his office. Scott was already there, sitting in a red leather chair in front of Garrison's big desk and bouncing one foot up and down impatiently. "About time," he said as his brother and sister came into the room.

Garrison was behind the desk looking over some documents. He glanced up and cleared his throat, obviously hoping to forestall any more hostility between the Hawthorne brothers. He motioned for Malcolm and Lorna to sit down, and when they had done so, he said, "I've been going over all the papers your father left behind, and I have to ask you a question."

"Go ahead," Malcolm said.

"Did Emmitt leave a will?"

Scott grunted. "You ought to know that better than we do. You were his lawyer."

"Yes, I was," Garrison said, "but he never had me draw up a last will and testament. I thought maybe he had written one and was keeping it at the ranch."

Malcolm looked at Lorna and Scott, both of whom shook their heads. He said, "If Dad did that, none of us knew anything about it."

"Well, this makes the situation, ah, rather more complicated. According to the laws of the state, when a man dies intestate, his property is divided equally among his heirs. That is, unless there's some sort of challenge—"

Scott stood up abruptly. "Well, there's going to be," he declared. "I don't mind sharing the profits, but I'll be damned if I'm going to share the responsibility with Malcolm. Somebody's got to be in charge."

Without knowing how he got there, Malcolm was on his feet, too. "I agree," he said. "Somebody's got to give the orders, and it's got to be somebody who knows what he's doing. That would be me."

Scott swung toward him. "You don't know anything except how to slap a brand on a cow! You'd run the ranch into the ground in a year!"

"You wouldn't even know which end of a cow to brand!" Malcolm shouted. "You sleep half the day, you stay drunk most of the time—"

"That's a damned lie!"

"Gentlemen, gentlemen!" Garrison said anxiously. "There's no need for this—"

"There's every need for it," Malcolm snapped as he swung toward the attorney. The very thing he had been afraid of when Todd Summers brought up the matter of the will had come about, but there seemed to be nothing Malcolm could do to stop it. Long-suppressed anger and resentment had boiled to the surface on both sides and burst like bubbles of foul-smelling swamp gas.

Malcolm leveled a finger at Scott and snarled, "He doesn't deserve any part of the ranch!"

"Now I get it!" Scott said. "You think since you were always Dad's favorite that you ought to get the whole thing and leave me and Lorna out of it. Well, you won't get away with it, you high-and-mighty bastard!"

"Scott!" Lorna gasped. She shot to her feet. "Both of you, stop it right now! What would Dad think—"

"I'm tired of worrying about what Dad would think," Scott growled. He clapped his hat on his head and turned toward the door. "You haven't heard the last of this," he warned Malcolm.

"Come back here, blast you!" Malcolm said. "You can't walk out on us—" He lunged after his brother and grabbed his shoulder.

Scott reacted immediately, whirling around and

launching a fist toward Malcolm's head. Seeing his brother about to hit him surprised Malcolm into immobility for a split second, long enough for the blow to crash into his jaw. The impact sent him staggering back against Garrison's desk as Lorna screamed and the lawyer shouted.

The punch hadn't really been that hard, just unexpected, and Malcolm rebounded quickly, leaping toward his brother and driving a fist into his stomach. He followed it with a left cross that sent Scott crashing against the door of the office. Scott nearly fell, but he caught his balance and threw himself at Malcolm with a hoarse, beastlike yell. They locked arms and sprawled on the rug in front of Garrison's desk, rolling around and slugging each other.

"Fetch the sheriff!" Garrison shouted to Lorna as he started around the desk. "I'll try to break them up!"

He reached for the struggling figures as the shaken Lorna dashed out of the office. A booted foot—it was impossible to tell in the tangle of arms and legs whose it was—lashed out and thudded into Garrison's ample belly. He moaned and stumbled backward, realizing that trying to intervene in this fight might not have been such a good idea after all.

Less than two minutes later, Sheriff Phil Brewster burst through the doorway, trailed by Lorna and Todd Summers. The sheriff's lean, mustachioed face was drawn in grim lines as he reached down and grabbed the first coat collar he could lay hold of. It happened to be Scott's, and Brewster was none too gentle as he jerked the young man up with surprising strength. A shove sent Scott staggering over to the desk, and as

The Hawthorne Legacy

Malcolm leapt to his feet, Brewster moved smoothly between the brothers. His six-gun was in his hand now, but he didn't threaten either of them with it. His voice was enough of a weapon.

"Stop it!" he bellowed. "Stop it right now, you two addlepated whelps! If your daddy was here, he'd wallop the both of you for fightin' like this! And him not gone even a week yet! If you got no respect for yourselves, then by God have some for Emmitt!"

"Talk to him," Malcolm said, breathing heavily as he gestured toward Scott. "He's the one who's gone crazy."

"Crazy, am I?" Scott demanded. He used the back of his hand to wipe away a thread of blood that had leaked from his nose. "Crazy to want what I've got coming to me?"

"You want the whole damned thing!"

"And I deserve it a hell of a lot more than you!"

Brewster looked at the lawyer and said, "Burt, I may have to let go with a couple of rounds into the ceilin' to shut these boys up, and if I do, I want you to charge 'em for the repairs." He pointed his pistol upward and eared back the hammer.

"That's all right, Sheriff," Malcolm said, still panting. "No need for any shooting. We'll get this straightened out."

"Yeah, but not now," Scott said as he bent over and picked up his hat. He jammed it on his head and glared at his brother. "I'll see you in court!"

With that, he turned and stalked out of the office, and this time Malcolm didn't try to stop him. Neither did anyone else.

Brewster let out a sigh that fluttered his mustache. "I was afraid of something like this happening, blast it. You boys never did learn how to get along."

Malcolm looked at Garrison. "What can Scott do about this? Can he really take the whole thing to court?"

The lawyer shrugged. "He can try to claim that he should be the sole heir, but I don't think he'll have a case. However, that won't stop him from causing a lot of trouble in the meantime."

"Can't you do something to stop him?" Lorna asked.

Garrison spread his hands and shook his head. "I wish I could, Lorna. But in the absence of a legal will, my hands are tied. I can't take either side in this dispute. We'll have to find a judge who can give the matter a fair and impartial hearing."

"Well, I hope you find him soon," Brewster muttered, "'cause if you don't, this whole town's gonna be a pot with the lid about to blow right off!"

Chapter Five

A heavyset, bearded man on an Appaloosa stallion rode into Delgado two weeks later, in the middle of the afternoon when most folks were taking their siesta. His brown eyes spotted the sign hanging over the door of the sheriff's office, and he nudged the big horse toward the boardwalk. He swung down from the saddle and looped the reins over the hitching post. There were two saddleboots on the rig, one holding a Winchester, the other a double-barreled greener, but the man left both weapons where they were. He didn't expect to run into any trouble in the sheriff's office.

Of course, a fella could never tell about such things. He'd learned that the hard way. As he looked around he patted the weapon holstered on his hip, a First Model LeMat two-barrel revolver. The gun, known also as the "Grape Shot Revolver," fired standard .42 caliber cartridges from its upper barrel and .63 caliber shotgun shells from the lower one. It wasn't as accurate as some, but it was good enough at close range.

The bearded man stepped up onto the boardwalk, crossed the planks, and pushed open the door.

Sheriff Phil Brewster was at his desk, a cup of coffee sitting beside the newspaper he was reading. When the door opened, he looked up and saw a stranger standing there. Glancing instinctively out the window, he spotted the Appaloosa tied up at the hitchrack. Nobody in Delgado rode such a horse. It was a fine-looking animal.

And considerably more impressive than its owner, Brewster thought as he eyed the stranger. The man was about medium height and broad all over, but a lot of his size appeared to be muscle. He wore khaki pants, a faded red bibfront shirt, and a long duster. A bandanna was tied around his neck under the dark beard that was shot with gray. His boots had seen plenty of wear, and judging by its walnut grips, so had the gun he carried. He lifted a hand and thumbed back the broad-brimmed Stetson he wore over thinning black hair.

"You'd be Sheriff Brewster?" the man asked.

The lawman nodded impatiently. "I got a badge on my chest, don't I? And the sign outside says this is the sheriff's office. I reckon you ought to be able to figure it out, mister."

"I like to be sure about these things." The man smiled and came across the room toward the desk. "Hear you've got yourself quite a legal tangle here in Delgado. Maybe I can help untwist it for you."

"How in blazes do you reckon that?" Brewster demanded. The idea that a drifter like this could be of any help in the mess plaguing the town was loco.

"My name's Earl Stark." The stranger extended his hand across the desk. "Judge Earl Stark."

"Judge?" exclaimed Brewster, his bushy gray eyebrows lifting in surprise.

"Yep. Federal Circuit Court for the Southwestern District." Stark grinned. "Pleased to meet you."

Brewster stood up and shook hands, still confused by this big stranger's claim. "I suppose you've got some bona fides?" he asked.

"Right here," Stark replied. He reached inside his duster and brought out a wad of documents from an inside pocket.

The sheriff took the papers and studied them for a long moment. They confirmed that the big man was who he said he was. Brewster handed them back and said, "Hope you don't mind me mentionin' it, Your Honor, but you don't look like no judge I ever saw."

"Wasn't always a judge," Stark grunted as he cached the papers in his duster again. "Before we get on with business, though, I've got a question for you." He brought out something else and thrust it toward Brewster. "Ever see this fella before?"

Brewster frowned. Stark was holding a torn photograph of a young man with a solemn yet somehow innocent face. The sheriff reached up to take the picture, then sensed that Stark didn't want to let go of it. He peered more closely at the image of the young man and shook his head. "Don't look familiar. What's his name, and how come you're lookin' for him?"

"Don't know his real name. He called himself the Kid. That's why I'm asking. I'm trying to find his kinfolk to inform them of his passing. He died . . . well, at the end of a rope. And for a good reason, of course, but I won't rest easy until I can find his people."

"I reckon I can't be of help. I'll keep it in mind, though. Light and set," Brewster invited as Stark put the photograph away. "I can fill you in on what's been happenin' around here." He settled back in the cracked leather chair behind the desk while Stark reversed one of the ladderbacks and straddled it. "Federal Circuit Court, you said? Sort of funny for a federal judge to be handlin' an inheritance dispute, ain't it?"

"Matters of inheritance generally fall under state statutes, all right," Stark agreed. "And I reckon the Hawthorne case would, too, if it wasn't such a powder keg. Judge Blandings over in Uvalde would normally hear it."

"That's what I figured. But Judge Blandings had to go to San Antone on account of his mama's real sick, or so I'm told."

"I wouldn't put her in the grave just yet," Stark said dryly. "The way I hear it, the judge doesn't want to touch this case. Emmitt Hawthorne was a powerful man in these parts, and whoever winds up running the Boxed H is liable to inherit the old man's influence along with the ranch."

Brewster's eyes narrowed as he reached for his pipe. "Are you sayin' Judge Blandings is duckin' the case 'cause he don't want to get on the bad side of whoever comes out on top in this wrangle?"

Stark shook his head and said, "I'm not claiming anything of the sort. But Harvey Blandings is no fool. With him out of the case, you'd expect it to be transferred to one of the other courts in this district, wouldn't you?"

"That's what I figured'd happen," Brewster replied. "Ain't got word yet who's goin' to handle it . . . until

The Hawthorne Legacy

you came ridin' in on that big Appaloosa, that is." He took out his tobacco pouch and began loading the bowl of the old briar.

Stark jerked a thumb at the coffeepot sitting on the stove in the corner. "Anything brewing in that?" he asked.

"Help yourself. I ain't makin' no claims as to how good my coffee is, though."

"I've drunk a heap of bad coffee at stage stations," Stark said as he stood up and ambled over to the stove, taking off his duster along the way and hanging it and his hat on a nail beside the door.

Brewster snapped his fingers. "Stage stations!" he echoed. "Now I savvy how come your name seemed a mite familiar at first. You used to ride shotgun on some of the stage lines up north of here. They called you Big Earl."

Stark nodded and picked up a chipped china cup from the top of the cabinet next to the stove. As he poured coffee in it, he said, "That's right."

"How in hell did a shotgun guard wind up a federal judge?" Brewster asked, overcome by curiosity. "Beggin' your pardon, Your Honor, for bein' so blunt about it."

With a chuckle, Stark returned to the chair. "Don't worry about it, Sheriff. The answer to your question is a long story, though, and we've got business of our own to tend to." He sipped the coffee, then nodded. "Not bad. Reckon it'd float a horseshoe, right enough." He set the cup on the desk and continued, "The reason you haven't heard anything about the Hawthorne case being scheduled for a hearing is that nobody wants to hear it. That's why the governor got in touch with me.

I swung by Austin on my way here, and he told me a little about the situation. Asked me to look into it as a favor."

"Well, I appreciate that, Your Honor, but I still don't see how a federal judge is going to try a case like this."

Stark grinned. "I didn't say it wouldn't be stretching things a little. But the Boxed H has a contract with the army to supply beef both for the troops and as rations for the reservations up in Indian Territory. That means the federal government has an interest in seeing that things settle down and start running smoothly on the ranch again. Otherwise the Boxed H is liable to default on its contract, and the army'll have to find somebody else to supply that beef on short notice. Could be some troopers and some Indians would go a mite hungry for a while if that was to happen. So in order to prevent that, I'm going to adjudicate the matter of Emmitt Hawthorne's inheritance."

Brewster let out a whistle. "Mighty slick," he said admiringly. "We get things settled around here, and you don't have to worry about either of the Hawthorne boys gettin' mad at you, since you don't answer to anybody this side of Washington City."

Stark picked up his coffee cup and raised it in a small salute to the lawman. "That's about the size of it," he said. "What I need now is for you to fill me in on everything that's happened since Emmitt Hawthorne's carriage fell into Espantosa Gorge."

"Some of it the governor's probably already told you."

"Tell me again," Stark said. "You were right here on the scene, and you might've noticed something they wouldn't know about in Austin."

The Hawthorne Legacy

Brewster nodded, got his pipe lit, and launched into a recitation of the facts as he knew them. Stark listened attentively, frowning when the sheriff described the fight between Malcolm and Scott Hawthorne in Burton Garrison's office. "This happened right after their father's memorial service?" he asked.

Brewster sighed. "Yep. Pitiful, ain't it? Thing is, it's gotten worse since then. Malcolm and Scott are at each other's throats the whole damned time. At least that's what Todd Summers tells me, and I reckon he ought to know since he's out at the Boxed H nearly every day."

"Who's Todd Summers? I don't recall that name from what the governor told me."

"He owns the biggest mercantile here in Delgado. Plans on marryin' up with Lorna Hawthorne. Todd's a good fella, and I sure hate to think what it'd've been like around the Boxed H if him and Lorna hadn't been there to keep those two wild brothers of hers in line at least some of the time."

"How does Miss Hawthorne feel about the whole inheritance situation?" asked Stark.

"She wishes it'd go away and leave 'em alone, I reckon," Brewster replied with another shake of his head. "She claims not to care one way or the other, as long as her brothers get along. Like I said, she's plannin' on gettin' hitched to Todd in a few months, and after the weddin', I suppose she'll move into town and live with him. He's got a nice little house over on Murphy Street."

"She doesn't care about her share of the ranch?" Stark sounded a little skeptical.

"Todd's business is pretty successful," Brewster pointed out. "I reckon Lorna's attached enough to the ranch to want to see it stay in the family, but knowin' her the way I do—and I've known her all her life—I figure she'd be happiest if Mal and Scott got along and ran things together."

"Sounds like the best solution to me." Stark finished the coffee in his cup, then asked, "And there's really no will?"

"None that we've been able to turn up. 'Course, the Boxed H ranch house is a mighty big place, with all sorts of nooks and crannies. Could be ol' Emmitt hid something out there and ain't anybody found it yet. But I wouldn't go to holdin' my breath and waitin' for a will to turn up."

Stark tugged distractedly on his short beard and frowned in thought. "Seems pretty cut and dried," he muttered, as much to himself as to Sheriff Brewster. "If Hawthorne died intestate, his holdings should be divided equally among his children. The law is simple and specific."

"Maybe so, but whoever wrote that law never knew Mal and Scott Hawthorne. Them boys got about as much use for each other as a pair of ol' tomcats. They swear they won't work together in the runnin' of the ranch, and if one of them gets control of it, I hate to think what the other one's liable to do—especially if it's Scott who gets left out."

Stark grunted. "Hotheaded, is he?"

"'Bout as hot as the hinges of Hades," Brewster said. "I'm sure as hell glad it's you who's got to straighten this out, Your Honor, and not me."

Stark nodded and stood up. "That's what I'm here for. Thanks for the coffee and the information."

"You're mighty welcome for both."

As he turned toward the doorway, Stark paused and looked back at Brewster. "Did you ever find Emmitt Hawthorne's body?"

"Nope."

"Then how do you know he's really dead?"

"Beggin' your pardon, Judge, but you ain't ever seen Espantosa Gorge or you wouldn't ask such a damn-fool question. It's three hundred feet deep, and the river at the bottom was runnin' fast that day. There's rocks all over the place that'd bust a man to little pieces if he landed on 'em." Brewster slowly shook his head. "Nope, there ain't no way in hell anybody could survive a fall like that, Your Honor."

"I'll take your word for it, Sheriff, but I'll want to have a look at the place anyway."

"Be glad to ride out there with you anytime you want. Repair work on the bridge is goin' along. Folks can use it again now if they're careful."

Stark took his duster and hat from the nail, put the hat on, and draped the duster over his left arm. "Where can I find Burton Garrison's office?"

"A block and a half down the street on the other side," Brewster told him.

"Thanks. I'll be seeing you, Sheriff."

Stark stepped out onto the boardwalk and shut the door behind him. He glanced up and down the street and saw that Delgado was stirring back to life following the afternoon siesta. People were moving around on the walks, and a wagon rumbled by on the street. The settlement looked like a pretty peaceful place.

Chances were, Stark reflected, it wasn't going to stay that way.

Chapter Six

Instead of going directly to Burton Garrison's office, Stark untied the Appaloosa from the hitchrack and led the horse back along the street toward a livery stable he had spotted coming into town. It was obvious he was going to be in Delgado for a few days, so he decided he might as well tend to his mount before continuing with the business that had brought him here.

He turned the Appaloosa over to the elderly but spry proprietor of the barn, who looked the animal over admiringly. "That's a lot of horse," the old man declared. "'Course, I reckon it takes a lot of horse for a gent like you."

Stark grinned. "We can't all be as scrawny as some folks I could mention, happen I wanted to get personal."

The old liveryman snorted, but his eyes sparkled

The Hawthorne Legacy

with enjoyment of the repartee. He slapped the Appaloosa lightly on the shoulder and said, "I'll take good care of this boy. You got my word on that, Mr. Stark."

With a deft motion Stark flipped a half-eagle into the air, and the stable owner caught the gold coin equally adroitly. Stark said, "I'll be back for my gear in a while," then lifted a finger to the brim of his hat and walked out of the barn, wincing a little as he left the cool shade of the building and felt the midday heat strike him again.

He turned west along Delgado's main street and passed the sheriff's office a moment later, continuing on toward a building he had already spotted. Like many other structures in this settlement on the edge of the desert, it was made of adobe, but it sported a plank boardwalk. Gilt letters painted on the front window announced GARRISON & PRENTICE, ATTORNEYS-AT-LAW.

Sheriff Brewster hadn't mentioned that Burton Garrison had a partner, but Stark wasn't surprised. Delgado was a bustling little town, and he was sure there was enough legal work here to keep at least two lawyers busy.

He stepped onto the boardwalk and opened the door without knocking, entering a small reception area divided from the rest of the office by a low wooden railing. Behind the desk on the other side of the rail sat a young woman. She looked up at Stark, smiled, and asked, "Yes? May I help you?"

Stark stopped in his tracks, taken aback by the woman's beauty. Her features were perfectly formed, and she had hair dark as a raven's wing that contrasted dramatically with her fair skin. Her eyes were a compelling blue-gray that reminded Stark of storm-tossed seas.

He realized that she had asked him a question, and before she was forced to repeat it, he said quickly, "I'm looking for Burton Garrison. Name's Earl Stark."

"Well, Mr. Stark, I'll check with Mr. Garrison and find out if he can see you now." She stood up, and Stark saw that she was fairly tall. She wore a white blouse with a few frills on the front and a dark brown skirt. The clothes were by no means as tight and revealing as a saloon girl's gaudy outfit, but Stark could still tell that she had a fine figure. He wondered what a woman this lovely was doing in Delgado, but he supposed that beauty could turn up anywhere, in the most unexpected places.

The young woman was about to open the door behind her desk when Stark added, "You'd best tell Mr. Garrison that I'm here to see him about the matter of Emmitt Hawthorne's estate."

She glanced over her shoulder at him, raising elegantly curved eyebrows. "Is that so? And what is your connection with that matter, Mr. Stark?"

He didn't see any reason to keep it a secret. If this gal was Garrison's secretary, chances were she'd find out all about it anyway. "It's Judge Stark. From the Federal Circuit Court for this district. I've come to Delgado to hear the case."

Her gray eyes flicked over his dusty trail garb and the revolver holstered at his hip, but if she thought he was crazy, he couldn't tell it from her expression. All she did was nod and say, "I see. I'll be right back." She opened the door, slid through gracefully, and closed it behind her.

While she was gone, Stark looked around the room. It was a typical frontier lawyer's office, with several cabinets in which files would be stored, a large calendar on one wall and a map of the state on another, a small wood-burning stove, and a massive bookcase. Stark opened the gate in the railing and ambled over to study the leather-bound volumes filling the shelves. There were several sets of legal commentaries, including Blackstone's, and some practical treatises such as White and Wilson's *Practice and Pleading,* which nearly every prairie-dog lawyer had in his library. There were books of history, as well, and even a few novels. Stark saw the Waverly books by Walter Scott and some scientific romances by that French fella, Jules Verne. Garrison obviously had some interest in the sciences, because books on such subjects as astronomy, handwriting analysis, and pharmacology were included. It was the sort of library that a well-educated, well-rounded man would possess.

The door to the other room opened, and Stark turned to see a thickset, white-bearded man emerge, followed by the young woman. The man extended his hand to Stark and said, "Judge Stark? I'm Burton Garrison. It's an honor to make your acquaintance."

Garrison didn't seem surprised by his visitor's appearance, and Stark guessed the woman had warned him. Taking the attorney's hand, he said, "The pleasure's mine, Counselor. I suppose you'd like to see my credentials."

"Well, yes, as a formality," Garrison said.

Stark took the documents from his duster and showed them to the lawyer, and he noticed the young woman taking an unobtrusive look at them as well. When Garrison was satisfied as to his identity, Stark went on, "Hope you don't mind that I didn't clean up before coming to see you. I'm anxious to get to the bottom of this Hawthorne business."

"Yes, Miss Prentice told me you've come to Delgado to conduct a hearing on the matter. A bit unusual for a federal judge to handle such a case, but we're certainly glad to have you here. I'm afraid things won't get back to normal in these parts until this dispute is settled, one way or the other."

Stark picked up a couple of things from Garrison's comments. One was a vestige of an eastern accent, which told him that Garrison wasn't a native Texan, although he had evidently been here quite some time. The other was the name Garrison had called the young woman—Miss Prentice. Stark glanced at the window, reading the words written there, which appeared backward from this side. "Garrison and Prentice," he said, switching his gaze to the woman. "Prentice would be you?"

"That's right," she said. "I'm Mr. Garrison's partner." A faint smile played around her wide mouth. "You must have taken me for a secretary."

"Well, as a matter of fact, I did," admitted Stark, somewhat embarrassed.

"No need to worry about it, Judge Stark," she told him crisply. "There aren't many female attorneys out here on the frontier, or anywhere else, for that matter. It's a perfectly understandable mistake. And to tell the truth, I *do* handle most of the secretarial chores for the practice, in addition to my other duties."

"I'd be lost without Jessica, I know that," Garrison said. "Come on into my office, Judge, and I'll tell you everything I can about the case."

The Hawthorne Legacy

"Thanks," Stark nodded. He looked at Jessica Prentice. "Are you coming, too?"

"Am I invited?" she asked coolly.

Stark tongued a front tooth to keep from grinning. He felt an instinctive liking for the young woman that didn't have anything to do with her beauty. Well, not *too* much, he amended. There was no denying her attractiveness. But she also seemed to be intelligent and quick-witted, two qualities that, in Stark's opinion, made any woman more appealing.

Besides, she might have noticed something about the Hawthorne case that Garrison had overlooked. Stark nodded and said, "Sure, I'd like to have you sit in on this parley."

Garrison tried to usher him into the inner office, but Stark stood back and gestured for Jessica Prentice to go first. She went in and sat in a red leather chair to one side of a huge desk. Garrison waited until Stark had settled into a morocco chair directly in front of the desk before he lowered himself into a similar chair behind it. Several piles of paper were spread out on the desktop, but Garrison shoved them aside.

"These other cases can wait," he said. "Tell me what you need to know, Judge Stark."

Stark took off his hat and perched it on his knee as he crossed his legs. "I got some of the facts from the governor when I was roped into this thing, and Sheriff Brewster told me some more. What I'd like for you to do, Counselor, is start at the beginning and tell me the whole story as you know it."

Garrison nodded. "I can do that, but you realize that most of what I can tell you is secondhand information. I didn't go out to the gorge where the bridge collapsed, nor was I with Sheriff Brewster when he informed the Hawthorne youngsters of their father's demise."

"That's all right," Stark assured him. "Just tell it the way you heard it."

Garrison did so, taking a little longer to cover the same ground Brewster had, but that was to be expected of a lawyer. Stark himself had fallen prey to a tendency toward long-windedness since he'd first hung his shingle back in Buffalo Flat, before he was appointed to fill a vacancy in the circuit court.

Jessica Prentice listened attentively to her partner's account of the case, and when Garrison wrapped things up, Stark turned to her and asked, "Do you have anything you'd like to add, Miss Prentice?"

She shook her head. "Burton was very comprehensive in his summation, Your Honor. And besides, I never had any dealings with Emmitt Hawthorne, or any of the other family members. Burton has been the family's attorney for many years. I've been handling some of our newer clients. Delgado has been growing quite steadily, you know."

"It may not keep growing if a war breaks out between Malcolm and Scott Hawthorne," Garrison growled. "And that's what's liable to happen after Judge Stark conducts his hearing."

"Why do you say that?" Stark asked.

"Because the law is clear on this matter. Emmitt died without a will, so there's no choice except to divide the estate equally."

"You're certain there's no will?"

"I never drew one up," Garrison declared emphatically. "I can't speak for what Emmitt might have done on his own, but he never said a word to me about writing up a will himself, and I think he would have told me." The attorney shook his grizzled head. "I wish he had, although the end result might have been the same if he divvied things up evenly."

"The two boys can't get along, eh?"

Garrison shook his head. "Those two have been scrapping for years, the sort of thing you expect from children but not from grown men."

"What if Emmitt Hawthorne had left the ranch to one of them and cut out the other?"

Garrison raised bushy white eyebrows in surprise at the question. "I don't think Emmitt would have done that," he said after a moment's thought. "Malcolm and Scott may have each thought that their father favored the other son, but I don't believe that was actually the case. I think he loved them equally, although it's no secret that Scott was something of a disappointment to him. That wouldn't change the way a man felt about his own son, though."

Stark wasn't so sure about that, but he didn't argue the point. "I'll hold the hearing as soon as possible. Does Delgado have a courthouse? I didn't notice one as I was riding in."

"No, I'm afraid not," Garrison replied. "Most of the county business is run out of the sheriff's office, although the tax assessor and collector has a separate office next door. There's a good-sized town hall down the street; I'm sure you could hold court there."

"All right. Will you notify the Hawthornes that I've come to town and that there'll be a hearing tomorrow morning at ten o'clock?"

"Certainly," Garrison agreed. "I'd be glad to."

"I can handle that for you, Burton," Jessica Prentice put in. "My horse could use some exercise. I could ride out to the Boxed H right now."

"Why, thank you, Jessica. I have to admit, that'll be easier than taking my buggy out there."

Stark looked at Jessica Prentice and commented, "So you're a rider, are you?"

"I learned to ride when I was quite young, Your Honor," she said. "There were stables near where I grew up in Philadelphia."

"Maybe you could show me some of the country around here before I leave," Stark heard himself saying. "Once the case is wrapped up, I mean."

"I could do that." Jessica's voice was friendly, but her expression was unreadable. "I've ridden over most of the area."

"Sounds good," Stark said as he stood up, holding his hat in front of him. "Might even pack a picnic lunch."

A smile appeared on Jessica's face again. "I like the sound of that even better."

Stark had surprised himself. Normally he would have preferred to wash off some of the trail dust and change into the sober black suit in his saddlebags before offering an invitation to a pretty young woman. But he had acted on impulse, and evidently it hadn't backfired on him. Which meant he'd better git while the gittin' was good, he decided. He put his hat on, ticked a finger against the brim, and said, "I'll see you folks later."

"Good day, Your Honor," Garrison said.

"Judge Stark," Jessica added with a nod.

Stark left them in the inner office and showed himself out. He headed toward the livery stable, intending to pick up his gear and rent a room in the hotel across the way. So far, what he had discovered in Delgado was exactly what the governor had warned him it would be. No matter what he decided at the estate hearing, somebody was going to be upset. Stark had never before let that possibility interfere with his enforcement of the law as he saw fit, and he wasn't going to start now.

No, the only real surprise so far was Miss Jessica Prentice, and Stark found himself almost wishing the Hawthorne case was more complicated than it was. Then he'd have an excuse to remain longer in Delgado and get to know her better.

Chapter Seven

Anytime something out of the ordinary was going on in a small town, word of it got around quickly, Stark knew. So he wasn't surprised when he reached the town hall with Burton Garrison and Sheriff Phil Brewster the next morning and found that everybody and his dog had shown up for the hearing.

"Hell's bells," Brewster muttered under his breath as the three men made their way along the boardwalk and through the crowd that thronged the entrance of the building. "I didn't figure there'd be this big a turnout."

"Emmitt Hawthorne was an important man," Garrison said, "and it's important to this town how his assets are disposed of. If the Boxed H prospers, so does Delgado."

Stark nodded. He had learned from his discussions with Brewster and Garrison the day before that there were other large ranches in the area—Wade Winthrop's Double W Bar chief among them—but none of the other cattlemen had developed anything comparable to Emmitt Hawthorne's far-flung spread.

The crowd parted in response to the sheriff's barked commands to let them through, and the three men made their way to the front of the hall, where a long table had been set up with chairs behind it. The rest of the big room was filled with chairs facing the table, most of which were already taken.

Stark presented a considerably different picture this morning. His hat was the same one he had sported on entering Delgado the day before, although he'd brushed the dust off it, but instead of the range garb, he wore a dark suit, white shirt, and gray vest. A string tie was knotted around his neck. He still wore the leather shell belt with the holstered LeMat.

He hung his hat on a rack on the side wall, then went to the center chair behind the table and pulled it back. Garrison took the seat to his right, Brewster the one to the left. Stark took a small black Bible from an inside pocket of his coat, along with his personal gavel, which had been carved for him by an old mountain man of his acquaintance. The old-timer had found it difficult to believe that the youngster who had even then been called Big Earl had grown up to be an honest-to-God judge; he'd offered the opinion that it was a step down from being a shotgun guard, but he had wished Stark the best anyway.

With his hand on the gavel, Stark hesitated before rapping the hearing to order and studied the crowd for a moment. Brewster noticed what he was doing and leaned over to whisper, "That's Malcolm and Lorna

Hawthorne, there in the front row. Don't see Scott yet."

Malcolm Hawthorne was a solid-looking young man who might have been handsome were it not for his grim expression. His sister, Lorna, who sat beside him, looked equally solemn. She was quite pretty, Stark thought, in a homespun sort of way. On her other side sat a dark-haired man in town clothes. Stark figured him for Todd Summers, Lorna's intended, from the way he was holding her hand and leaning over from time to time to whisper to her. She nodded whenever he spoke.

Clustered around the Hawthornes were several cowboys, who had probably cleaned up a mite for this trip into town but who still looked unmistakably like ranch hands. Stark asked Brewster in a low voice, "Is that the Boxed H crew?"

"Some of 'em," the sheriff replied. "Don't see all of the hands, though, and that ain't a good sign. I been hearin' that some of 'em have lined up behind Scott, while the others figure Mal's the best man to run the ranch."

Stark glanced at the lawman. "I thought you said Malcolm was the foreman. Stands to reason all the crew would back him."

"'Cept the ones he's had a fallin' out with in the past, fellas he threatened to fire if they gave him any more trouble. There's always some o' that kind in every big crew."

"I wonder where Scott is," Garrison muttered. "I hear he's been staying in town as much as at the ranch lately, but I'm sure he knows about this hearing. Jessica informed him personally, she said."

Stark glanced toward the rear of the room. Jessica Prentice was sitting there, and she smiled when she noticed him looking at her. Stark returned the smile briefly and then turned his attention back to the matter at hand.

He had just picked up the gavel when the crowd at the back of the room began to stir. Many spectators had been forced to stand because there weren't enough chairs, and they parted abruptly as two men strode in, followed by several others. One of the newcomers was a young man with carefully barbered blond hair, dressed in a good brown suit. His companion was bigger, rangier, and more rugged looking and wore a duster much like Stark's, open and pushed back on the right side to allow him easy access to the well-worn walnut grips of the revolver holstered on his hip. His hair was long and pale, his lantern-jawed face set in a taut mask. Stark didn't like him on sight.

"Son of a bitch," Brewster breathed beside him. "I hope that ain't who I think it is."

Stark had already figured out a few things from the crowd's reaction. "The young man's Scott Hawthorne, isn't he?" he asked in a low voice.

Brewster nodded. "That's Scott, right enough."

Garrison leaned forward. "Who's that with him?"

"Name's Cahoon, I think. Seen posters on him in the past, though they've all been withdrawn now. Some slick, no-account lawyer got him off on all the charges against him, no offense to either of you gents."

"Gunman, is he?" grunted Stark.

"He hires out," Brewster said. "And he's a bad 'un, from what I hear. Those boys who came in behind Scott are the rest of the Boxed H hands, the ones who figure to support him."

"I thought as much," Stark said.

The excited murmurs of the crowd quieted some as

Scott Hawthorne and the man called Cahoon reached the front row of chairs. After exchanging a cold stare with his brother for a second, Scott said something to two of the townsmen seated down the row from Malcolm and Lorna. The townies vacated the chairs rapidly and headed for the back of the room, and Scott and Cahoon sat down. Stark bristled at the arrogance of the move. Scott obviously thought he could waltz in here with a hired gun at his side and get whatever he wanted.

Well, by God, he'd find out things didn't work that way in Earl Stark's court.

Stark slapped the gavel down against the tabletop once, twice, three times. An expectant silence filled the room. As he felt the eyes of the crowd on him, Stark looked over at Brewster and nodded.

The sheriff rose to his feet and said in a loud voice, "This hearing is now in session, the Honorable Judge Earl Stark presidin'." He glanced at Stark. "You want 'em all to stand up?"

Stark shook his head. "I'm here already, and I never have held with too much ceremony. Sit down, Sheriff, and thanks."

Brewster settled back in his chair, and Stark laid the gavel down and swept his gaze over the packed room. "This hearing is for the purpose of disposing of the estate of one Emmitt Hawthorne. I've spoken to Sheriff Brewster about Mr. Hawthorne's death, and I've discussed the state of his legal affairs with his attorney, Mr. Garrison. I'm prepared to issue a ruling, but before I do, I want to give anyone who so desires the opportunity to speak concerning this case. I warn you, this will be done in an orderly fashion, but if anyone here has any facts to present—"

Stark had been expecting a race, and he got one. Malcolm and Scott both shot to their feet and started talking at once. Stark didn't let them get very far. He smacked the gavel sharply against the tabletop, silencing them.

"I said we were going to proceed in an orderly fashion," he warned, pointing the gavel at each of them in turn. He considered for a few seconds, then nodded to Malcolm. "You first."

Scott opened his mouth and seemed ready to protest that decision, but a cold glance from Stark made him shut up and sit down. Malcolm nodded to the judge, then reached inside his coat and took out a folded piece of paper. He said, "Thanks for listening to me, Your Honor, and I'm sorry there's been so much trouble the past few weeks. Truth to tell, there's not really any need to go ahead with this hearing."

"What do you mean by that?" asked Stark.

Malcolm took a deep breath. "I found this paper at the ranch this morning, stuck back behind a broken board in a cubbyhole in my dad's desk. You can see for yourself, Judge, it's a will leaving the Boxed H to me."

The stunned silence following that announcement lasted only a few seconds. Then an uproar broke out that filled the courtroom. Stark's eyes widened in surprise. He hadn't expected any such development as this. Scott Hawthorne was on his feet again, shouting at his brother in disbelief, and Malcolm was yelling right back at him. The Boxed H crew members who were supporting their foreman let out a cheer, then began shouting jeers at the hands who backed Scott. The citizens of Delgado, who thus far had been carefully neutral, were babbling excitedly. Stark watched them for a moment, then glanced at Jessica Prentice, who was exchanging a shocked look with her law partner. It was clear neither she nor Garrison had known anything about this purported last will and testament of Emmitt Hawthorne.

Stark allowed matters to run their course for about a minute, then hammered on the table with the gavel. It took a while to calm things down, even with Brewster on his feet shouting for order. The only person in the room who didn't seem shaken up by Malcolm's announcement was the gunman called Cahoon, who was still sitting calmly in the first row. Stark figured he wasn't going to get excited about anything unless he had been paid to do so.

Finally, as Stark was about to tell Brewster to fire a couple of shots into the ceiling to get folks' attention, the crowd began to settle. Stark rapped the gavel some more, and most of the spectators stopped talking and sat down. But Malcolm and Scott were still going at it, nose to nose, and their sister was trying to get between them. Stark gave up on the gavel and roared, "Shut up!"

Malcolm and Scott both glanced at him and saw that he had risen to his feet. Stark was an imposing figure, and his bearded face was flushed with anger. He pointed a finger at them and demanded, "You boys ever heard of contempt of court? You're about to find out all about it!"

Grudgingly, Scott backed away from his brother and

sat down. Malcolm was about to do the same when Stark motioned curtly to him.

"Bring that paper up here," he ordered. "I want to take a look at it."

Malcolm obliged, slapping the document down on the table in front of Stark. The judge picked it up and with his other hand took a pair of spectacles from his vest pocket and settled them on his nose. The will was a single sheet of heavy paper, folded once, the words scrawled on it in dark blue ink. There was no heading save for the time-honored opening words:

> *"I, Emmitt Hawthorne, being of Sound Mind and Body, do make this my Last Will and Testament...."*

Stark's practiced eye scanned the rest of it quickly. Garrison was on his feet, reading over Stark's shoulder, as was Brewster on the other side.

"Good God Almighty," the lawman said in a hushed voice.

Stark glanced up at Lorna Hawthorne. "You'd better come up here, miss," he told her quietly, then looked at Scott. "You, too."

Scott got to his feet, as did Cahoon. Before the gunman could step forward with his employer, Stark snapped, "Just you, Hawthorne. Leave your lapdog where he is."

Cahoon's eyes narrowed with hostility. Stark didn't care. He'd seen Cahoon's kind before, and he had no use for the breed.

Scott and Lorna came up to the table. Stark put away

his spectacles, then turned the document around so that they could read it for themselves. "The terms are pretty simple," he told them. "You receive a legacy of four thousand dollars, ma'am, and your brother Scott gets two thousand. Everything else goes to Malcolm Hawthorne."

"Two thousand dollars!" Scott burst out. "Two thousand! That old bastard! It's not possible!" A shrewd look appeared in his eyes. He jabbed a finger at the will and went on, "It's *not* possible. That will's nothing but a fake!"

"I found it right where I said I did," Malcolm insisted.

"Yeah, and you probably put it there!" Scott shot back at him. "Come on, Your Honor, you can't possibly believe this . . . this pathetic little trick!"

"What do you think, Miss Hawthorne?" Stark asked Lorna.

She was biting her lower lip, and her face was pale beneath the bonnet she wore. "I . . . I'm surprised Dad did this," she finally said. "But it looks like his handwriting, and I wouldn't want to go against his wishes."

Stark looked at Burton Garrison. "What about it?" he asked the attorney. "Is that Emmitt Hawthorne's writing?"

Garrison held out a hand. "May I see the document?"

Stark gave it to him, and for several long, tense moments, Garrison studied what was written on it. Then he sighed, returned the paper, and said, "As far as I can tell—and I've seen plenty of examples of it over the years—that's Emmitt Hawthorne's hand. I'm as surprised as anyone by the terms, but it's my opinion he wrote that will."

"But that can't be legal!" Scott protested. "A man can't write up his own will, can he? Doesn't he have to have a lawyer do it?"

Stark shook his head. "Not in these parts. A will like this is perfectly legal and legitimate in Texas. Now, you folks go sit down. I've got to issue a ruling."

"You can't!" Scott howled. "You haven't heard my side of it!"

"There aren't any sides any more," Stark told him. "There's only Emmitt Hawthorne's wishes to consider now."

Lorna and Malcolm went back to their seats, and Scott followed suit a moment later, still looking stricken and muttering under his breath.

Stark picked up the gavel and said, "It's the finding of this court that the last will and testament of Emmitt Hawthorne is valid and binding, and that under the terms of said document, Miss Lorna Hawthorne will receive a bequest of four thousand dollars. Mr. Scott Hawthorne will receive a bequest of two thousand dollars. The balance of Emmitt Hawthorne's estate goes to Malcolm Hawthorne." Stark rapped the gavel on the table. "This hearing is adjourned!"

All of the spectators got to their feet immediately. Scott confronted Malcolm again, vowing, "You won't get away with this, you son of a bitch! You're trying to steal that ranch right out from under me!"

"You don't even deserve what you got," Malcolm grated. "Now get out of my way." He tried to push past his furious brother.

Scott's anger exploded, and he swung a fist at Malcolm's head. Stark saw the blow before it landed and yelled, "Hold on there!" but it was too late. Scott's fist crashed against Malcolm's jaw, rocking the older brother's head back sharply. Scott bored in as Malcolm staggered.

Malcolm righted himself quickly, however, ducked Scott's next punch, and stepped closer to hook a hard right of his own into Scott's midsection. Lorna was pleading with them to stop fighting, but her cries were lost in the uproar that was sweeping through the room. All over the town hall, fights were breaking out as the wild young cowboys from the Boxed H took sides in the conflict. Some of the townspeople were drawn into the brawl as well, but most fled to the exits.

Brewster yelled for order as he hurried out from behind the table, but no one paid attention. Stark followed him. He was worried about Cahoon; the gunman might take advantage of this ruckus to try to put a bullet in Malcolm Hawthorne and appeal Stark's ruling with lead. But he spotted Cahoon sidling away from the center of the fracas, apparently willing to bide his time.

One of the brawlers stumbled against Stark. Catching the man by the shirt collar and the back of the belt, Stark heaved him off his feet and propelled him over the table, causing Garrison to scamper out of the way. Somebody else threw a punch at Stark and missed, and Stark made sure the man didn't get a second chance. He brought a clubbed fist down on top of the man's head, crushing his hat and sending him sprawling to the floor, stunned. Stark stepped over him, grabbed hold of two more men, and cracked their skulls together. They fell limply when he dropped them.

Stark found himself smiling a little. It had been a while since he'd been in a good fight.

A scattergun went off with a deafening roar, and bits of plaster rained down from the ceiling where the charge of buckshot had penetrated.

"Hold it!" Sheriff Brewster bellowed. "I got another barrel in this greener, and I don't mind usin' it!"

Stark's smile became a grin. He wasn't sure where Brewster had gotten the shotgun, but it had put an end to the fight in a hurry. The brawlers were standing around as if they'd been frozen in a blue norther, stupid looks on their faces. Stark realized he shouldn't be grinning and made himself look solemn and angry again. Hell, he *was* mad. Here he'd issued a nice, simple ruling, and all Hades had broken loose.

"The next man who throws a punch goes to jail!" he shouted.

"And I ain't liable to let him out anytime soon," added Brewster. "You boys oughta be ashamed of yourselves!"

Malcolm and Scott Hawthorne were both disheveled, and Scott had a bloody scrape on one cheek. Several of the other men were battered and bruised, but that was the extent of the injuries. Stark was glad there hadn't been any gunplay.

"Take your boys and ride on out of town," he warned Scott. "I don't want to hear about you causing any more trouble."

"I didn't cause *this* trouble," Scott said. "He's the one who stole the ranch from me." He glowered at his brother.

"There'll be no more of that," Stark snapped. "Get moving, and take your 'friend' with you." He looked meaningfully at Cahoon, who was standing to one side, seemingly bored by the whole affair.

Scott bent and picked up his hat, which had gotten stepped on in the melee. As he brushed it off he said to Malcolm, "I'll pack my things and be off the ranch by the time you get there."

Lorna put a hand on his arm. "I'm sure you don't have to do that—"

"I want to," Scott told her. "You don't think I'd stay under the same roof as that snake any longer, do you?" He patted his sister's shoulder. "Sorry about all this, Lorna. I never thought Mal would stoop so low."

With that, he turned and stalked out of the town hall, followed by Cahoon and the hands who had supported his cause.

"I'm sorry, too, Lorna," Malcolm said. "I knew Scott would be upset, but I was hoping he'd listen to reason."

"Neither of you listens to reason where the other one is concerned," Lorna said bitterly. She turned to the dark-haired young man beside her. "Let's go, Todd. I don't want to be here anymore."

Todd Summers escorted her out of the building, and Malcolm followed a moment later, a glum look on his face. Malcolm had won, Stark thought, but he had lost at the same time.

Maybe the Boxed H was big enough to make up for the loss of a brother.

Chapter Eight

The town hall cleared out quickly after the Hawthornes left. Some of the spectators might have hoped the fight between the brothers and their backers would spill out into the street, but Sheriff Brewster hurried outside to make sure that didn't happen. As Stark sat at the table, putting away his Bible and gavel, Jessica Prentice came to the front of the room and said to her partner, "What do you think of that will Malcolm Hawthorne found, Burton?"

Garrison shrugged as he stood up. "You heard my opinion, Jessica. I believe the document is in Emmitt's writing and is therefore valid. But I'm as shocked as Scott that Emmitt would do such a thing."

"What about the girl?" Stark asked. "Hawthorne pretty much cut her out, too. Four thousand dollars isn't much considering what I've heard about the value of the Boxed H."

"True enough," Garrison agreed. "But as I mentioned before, Emmitt knew that Lorna is engaged to marry Todd Summers. Perhaps he thought he didn't need to provide any more for her than the bequest he allowed."

Stark pushed himself to his feet. "Well, my job's done. Didn't amount to much, after all."

Jessica turned to face him and said, "I hope you won't be leaving Delgado before I get that chance to show you around."

"I'm in no hurry to get back on the trail," Stark said with a grin. "How's tomorrow morning sound to you?"

"It's fine with me . . . if Burton has no objection to my taking some time off from the office."

Garrison waved a meaty hand. "You young people go ahead and have your picnic or whatever you've got in mind. The office can get along for one day without you, Jessica."

"Thank you." She smiled at Stark. "We have a date, then."

"Yep. I reckon we do."

Jessica went out with Garrison, discussing the Hawthorne case, as Stark went to the hat rack to get his Stetson. He was reaching for it when an unfamiliar voice behind him said, "Hell of a ruckus, warn't it?"

Stark looked over his shoulder and saw an old man standing there, hands tucked in the hip pockets of ragged denim pants. The old-timer wore suspenders over the faded red top of his long underwear, and a battered hat with a pushed-back front brim perched on his thatch of white hair. A bushy, grizzled beard stuck out from his face at odd angles.

Stark nodded. "Yes, it was."

"Thought them Hawthorne boys was goin' to kill

each other, the way they was goin' at it." The old man stuck out a gnarled paw. "They call me Nat."

Stark shook hands with him. "Earl Stark."

"I know. You was the judge. I seen the whole thing, you know, from the back of the room there."

"Good," grunted Stark. He put his hat on and started toward the door.

The garrulous old-timer fell in step beside him. "Just got to Delgado this mornin'," he said. "Been lookin' for gold down south of here, 'twixt the mountains and the Rio Grande. Didn't find nary a speck o' color, though."

"Too bad," Stark said, only half listening.

"Figgered I might as well come up here and see what life in the big city's like. Wonder if it's always this excitin'."

Stark had to smile. Only an old desert rat like Nat, who might not have seen another living creature except his mule and a few lizards for months on end, would consider Delgado a big city.

"Planning on staying around for a while, are you?" Stark asked as they stepped out onto the boardwalk.

"I sure might. Want to see what else is goin' to happen."

On impulse Stark asked, "How about a drink?"

Nat wiped the back of his hand across his mouth and grinned shrewdly. "Well, I couldn't very well say no to an invite from a judge, now, could I? Wouldn't want to be charged with that, what do you call it, content of court?"

Stark didn't bother correcting him. A drink was probably what he'd been after all along, and Stark didn't begrudge him that. He angled his head toward the Red Horse Saloon and said, "Come on."

The hitchrack in front of the saloon was full. Stark saw the Boxed H brands on most of the horses tied there. When he and Nat entered, he looked around and spotted Scott Hawthorne at the far end of the bar. The young man's elbows were planted on the hardwood as he threw back shots of whiskey. Cahoon stood beside him, while the Boxed H hands who had been on his side in the dispute were ranged along the bar. There was no sign of Malcolm or Lorna, and Stark figured they had gone back to the ranch.

Nat hesitated inside the batwings and rubbed a hand through his scruffy beard. "You don't reckon there'll be any more trouble whilst we're havin' that drink, do you?"

Scott Hawthorne didn't seem to be paying attention to anything but the whiskey in his glass. Stark said, "There won't be any trouble."

He led Nat over to an empty table and gestured for him to sit down. Nat did so, practically licking his lips in anticipation as he glanced at the sparkling array of bottles on the backbar, below the long mirror. "I sure 'preciate this, Yer Honor," he said.

"You're welcome, Nat." Stark sat down and signaled to the bartender. The man sent a young woman in a spangled dress over to the table, and she gave them a big smile.

"What'll it be, gents?" she asked as she pushed back a strand of red hair from her face.

"Little early in the day for anything except beer for me," Stark told her. "As cold as you've got. As for my friend here . . . ?"

"Whiskey?" Nat asked tremulously. "Maybe some o' that there Maryland rye?"

Stark nodded to the girl, and she said, "Coming right up, gentlemen." She hurried back to the bar.

Nat started talking about the time he had spent prospecting in the desert to the south, but Stark paid little attention to him except to nod and say "Uh-huh" every once in a while. Mostly he was watching Scott Hawthorne, who kept muttering to Cahoon and tossing back drinks. The boy was sure enough getting drunk, Stark thought, maybe working up some liquid courage for whatever he planned to do about the will. Not that there was anything Scott could do, at least not legally. The Boxed H belonged to Malcolm Hawthorne now, fair and square.

But Scott had made it plain he didn't intend to let that judgment stand. Whether he would calm down eventually and see the futility of going against the law, Stark couldn't say. But there was every possibility the trouble was only beginning, not ending.

It might be a good idea for him to stay around Delgado for a few days, Stark mused. There could be further need for a judge, and since he had been in charge of the initial hearing, it made sense for him to retain jurisdiction.

Besides, that would provide the excuse he needed to spend a little more time with Jessica Prentice.

Suddenly he became aware that Nat was staring at him. "Sorry," Stark said. "Reckon my mind must've wandered. What were you saying?"

"Just askin' what you thought that boy and his pet gunman was goin' to do next."

"Don't know," Stark replied honestly. "But I've got a feeling it won't be long before we find out."

* * *

Stark nursed his beer at the Red Horse until Scott Hawthorne, Cahoon, and the Boxed H hands had left, galloping out of town in the opposite direction from the ranch. Stark wasn't sure where they were going, but at least they weren't on their way to a direct confrontation with Malcolm. He dropped coins on the table to pay for the drinks, slapped Nat on the shoulder, and left the old-timer there to finish his whiskey.

Delgado had gotten back to normal quickly, at least on the surface. But as Stark spent the rest of the day strolling around the settlement and talking to the townspeople, he could sense an undercurrent of tension in the air. Range wars had broken out before over much smaller stakes. Stark spent a couple of hours in the sheriff's office, talking to Brewster and going through his wanted posters to find out more about Cahoon, but there was no outstanding paper on him. Brewster said he'd heard that Cahoon had been tried and acquitted a few times in another county. Stark asked him to find out where. The lawman was clearly worried.

The evening and the night passed quietly, however, and after a breakfast at the Plateau Café—during which Stark put away a big stack of flapjacks, half a dozen eggs, three thick slices of ham, and an entire pot of coffee—he ambled over to the law offices of Burton Garrison and Jessica Prentice and found the attorneys working.

Jessica gathered up her papers and put them away in one of the cabinets. "I wasn't sure when you would want to start on our ride," she told Stark, "so I thought I'd get a little work done while I was waiting."

"Good idea." He was wearing the dark suit he'd worn

the day before. It was all right for riding, although it was more comfortable to wear in a courtroom. He also continued to wear the shell belt with its holstered LeMat. He would have felt too uncomfortable riding out of town without it, even though he would also have the Winchester and the greener.

Jessica looked lovely, Stark thought, in a dark green riding outfit consisting of a short-waisted jacket and a long, split skirt. The lacy front of a silk blouse peeked out from under the jacket. Her dark hair was pulled loosely behind her head and spilled down her back. She picked up a dark brown, flat-crowned hat from her desk and put it on, pulling the strap taut under her chin. If not for her fair skin, Stark thought, she would have looked like the daughter of some wealthy Mexican grandee.

She smiled at him. "Shall we go? My horse is down at the livery stable."

"So's mine." Stark linked his arm with hers. "So long, Mr. Garrison."

"Yes, good-bye, Burton," Jessica said brightly.

Garrison chuckled as he lifted a hand in farewell. "Looking at you two sure makes a man wish he were young again," he said wistfully.

As they stepped outside and started toward the stable, Stark said, "I'm not all that young, you know, no matter what your partner says. Shoot, I'm probably nigh old enough to be your father."

"I don't believe that for a moment, Your Honor," Jessica said.

"Why don't you call me Earl?"

"But wouldn't that be disrespectful?" she asked in a tone of mock surprise. "After all, you *are* a judge."

"I've been called a lot worse," Stark told her with a grin. "One old boy compared me to a hog of his, and another said I was nothing but a low-down skunk. Why, one time a fella called me—"

"I think I get the idea," Jessica said hastily before Stark could warm up to his subject. "I'd be happy to call you Earl. And I'm Jessica, not Miss Prentice or ma'am."

"That's fine with me, Jessica."

They reached the livery barn, and as the hostler saddled up their mounts, Stark wondered again at his impulsive behavior. He'd had a few lady friends now and then, in the time since the death of the woman he had hoped to marry, but rarely had he been as forward with any of them as he'd been with Jessica Prentice. On the other hand, he thought, he hadn't been as intrigued by any of them, either.

They rode out of town a few minutes later, heading west, Stark mounted on the big Appaloosa and Jessica riding a fine-looking chestnut mare. She rode astride—no sidesaddle for her, she had said emphatically—and Stark admired the way she handled the mare. Obviously she had spent a lot of time at those riding stables back in Philadelphia when she was a girl.

When they had left Delgado behind and were trotting down the road to Harker's Crossing, Stark said, "Not to mix too much business with pleasure, but I'd like to take a look at that bridge where Emmitt Hawthorne fell into the gorge."

Jessica nodded. "I knew you'd want to see the place. We'll ride out there, then take a look at the Boxed H." She patted the saddlebags that had been thrown over the back of the chestnut. "And later we'll have that picnic you mentioned."

They kept their pace easy and took about an hour to reach Espantosa Gorge. The sound of hammering reached their ears before they came within sight of the gorge itself. When they got there, Stark wasn't surprised to see that the repair work was still going on. New support timbers had been sunk on the south side of the bridge, and most of the crossbeams had been installed. A new plank flooring was going down now. Once that was done, the final step would be to replace the railing along the south side. A man on foot or horseback could cross the bridge now, but only with great care, for several large gaps remained.

"Want to cross here?" Stark asked Jessica as they reined in their horses and looked out over the gorge.

A tiny shudder went through her. "I don't think so. I'd prefer to wait until all the work is done. It's supposed to be completed within another three weeks or so. Until then, I'd rather go around the long way."

"Fine by me," Stark replied. He left unsaid the fact that taking the longer route would give him more time with her. He studied the bridge for a moment. "Hawthorne was headed this way over the gorge when the bridge went, right?"

Jessica nodded. "That's the way I understand it. He was on his way to town from the ranch, so he must have been coming in this direction. They found the horse and the wrecked carriage on a shelf at the bottom of the gorge on this side."

Stark nodded slowly, turning over in his mind everything he had heard about the accident. "Sheriff

Brewster thinks something knocked out a support or two on the south side, and that caused the bridge to collapse. Hawthorne must have felt the bridge going and tried to whip up enough speed from his horse to get off on this side before it fell. He didn't quite make it, though."

"And when he fell, his body plunged into the river and was washed away," Jessica finished. "That theory has been accepted by Sheriff Brewster and my partner, and to tell the truth, I believe it, too. Otherwise, Mr. Hawthorne's body would have been found somewhere." She nodded grimly toward the defile. "He certainly couldn't have survived such a fall."

"Nope," agreed Stark. "Anybody who fell into that gorge would sure enough be dead, all right." He changed the subject by saying, "Those carpenters who're repairing the bridge—are they being paid by the county?"

"That's right. The county is responsible for the road and the bridge, even though all the land you can see over there on the other side belongs to the Boxed H. The county has a right of way through the ranch for the road. I had nothing to do with it, of course, since all the papers were drawn up long before I ever came to Delgado, but Burton could tell you about it. He handled the matter for Mr. Hawthorne, as well as for the county."

Stark looked at her. "Garrison represented both parties to the agreement? That's a mite unusual, isn't it?"

"Not where there's only one lawyer for over two hundred miles. You forget, Judge Stark—I mean, Earl—this part of the state was largely unsettled back then. It was only after the road was put in that Delgado and Harker's Crossing began to grow."

"I've seen that happen before," Stark said. He edged his horse forward, peered over the edge into the gorge for a moment, then turned away. "We might as well ride on to the Boxed H."

"I have to admit, that place makes my blood run cold," Jessica said as they trotted along the eastern edge of the gorge, keeping well back from the rim. "It's not that Mr. Hawthorne died there. I don't like places where the sun never shines, like the bottom of that gorge."

"Can't say as I blame you," Stark said. "It's a mighty long drop."

For the next hour, as they rode to the northern end of the gorge and crossed the river there, then angled southwest toward the Boxed H headquarters, they put the subject of Emmitt Hawthorne's death behind them. Stark was more interested in finding out about Jessica, and she obliged by telling him of her life as the daughter of a well-to-do banker in Philadelphia.

"My poor mother died giving birth to my brother when I was eight. Since my father was away most of the day, we were raised by nannies, though I sometimes felt I was more of a mother to my brother than a sister. I was always an independent child, and my mother's death made me even more determined to make my own way. After hearing my father talk about lawyers so much, I decided I wanted to become one.

"I went to law school at Radcliffe," she went on, "even though my father was scandalized at first when I told him I wanted to be an attorney. He had thought that after I graduated from Miss Esmeralda's Finishing School my education would be over. I'm sure he expected me to marry one of the up-and-coming young men from his bank. Quite a few of them courted me."

"I'll bet they did," Stark told her. "A beautiful girl

with a rich banker for a daddy draws beaus like flies to molasses."

She laughed. "Thank you . . . I think. At any rate, Father found out how determined I was, and, well, he never could refuse me anything I really wanted. I should be ashamed to say it, but I had the poor man wrapped totally around my finger."

"Had him buffaloed, we'd call it out here."

"I like that," Jessica said brightly. "Yes, I had my poor father buffaloed." Her expression became more serious as she went on, "It wasn't as easy once I actually started practicing law, though. Most people aren't accustomed to the idea of a female attorney, even in this day and age."

"I reckon not. To be honest, Jessica, you're the first one I've run across. Is that what brought you out here—more of an opportunity to practice law?"

"That and a desire to see the West. When I saw the advertisement Burton placed in one of the law journals seeking a partner for his practice, something told me I had to take that job. I haven't regretted it since. And Burton's been wonderful about giving me a chance. He's an old bachelor, you know, and I suspect he thinks of me as the daughter he never had."

"I expect you're right," Stark said. From what he'd seen, he figured she had Burton Garrison as buffaloed as she did her old daddy back in the City of Brotherly Love. "How much courtroom experience have you had?"

"Oh, not too much as yet. There were too few people who trusted my abilities enough to let me handle their affairs—strictly because of my gender. I finally had to go into practice with five others, all of them men, but they invariably assigned me the more mundane tasks. I was even expected to make their coffee for them!" She changed the subject to his background by asking, "Where did you go to law school?"

"Well . . . I'm afraid I don't have the formal training you do. Most of my lawyering I learned from a set of books I found on one of the stagecoaches I was guarding."

She looked at him in surprise. "You were a stagecoach guard?"

He nodded. "Rode shotgun on many an old Concord for about ten years. Before that I punched cattle and did a little scouting for the army, back in the Red River War. But I decided I wanted to do something more with my life than shoot desperadoes, so when I got hold of those law books, I started studying. Got admitted to the bar a while back, then later I was appointed judge. The attorney general said they needed a fella who had some experience out here to handle the southwestern district."

Stark didn't mention the other things he'd learned after his appointment—that judges in this part of the country tended to meet a violent end, that nobody else had really wanted the job, and that the congressman who'd wangled the appointment for him had really been settling an old score against him. But so far, things had worked out all right.

There were other things about his life he didn't bring up, either—things he wasn't particularly proud of. Given the nature of his job, he figured he and Jessica would never get to know each other well enough to get into that part of his history. A fella never knew, though.

They were already on Boxed H land, had been ever since crossing the Espantosa. Stark reined in before they reached the ranch house, preferring not to pay a visit to Malcolm and Lorna Hawthorne quite yet. "Just wanted to take a look at the place," he explained to Jessica as they sat their horses on a ridge overlooking the ranch headquarters. "It wouldn't look right for me to get too friendly with these folks after I decided a case they were involved in."

"I imagine being a judge forces you to keep your distance sometimes when you'd prefer not to," she said, watching him.

Stark met her eyes. "That it does. But not all the time."

He let that lie and turned his attention back to the ranch. He knew from his own days as a cowboy the signs of a successful operation, and the Boxed H displayed all of them. The corrals looked tight and strong, the barns were well cared for, and the small vegetable gardens were as productive as they could be in this semi-arid climate. The house was an impressive sight, with its rambling size and mix of architectural styles.

Some of the hands spotted them on the ridge and rode over to check on them. The cowboys tugged off their hats when they realized one of the riders was a woman. "Howdy, Miss Jessica," a cowboy said. "What can we do for you?"

"We're just visiting. Judge Stark here wanted to take a look at the ranch."

The spokesman for the hands grinned at Stark. "Howdy, Judge. We'll go tell Mal and Miss Lorna that you're here. I reckon they'll ask you to stay to dinner."

Stark shook his head. "Thanks, but that's not necessary. Miss Prentice and I have to be getting back to town. Please tell the Hawthornes that we came by."

"Sure will. You certain you don't want to ride on down to the ranch house?"

Stark shook his head and turned his horse. "Thanks anyway," he called over his shoulder.

As Jessica and he rode back toward the river, they found they had company. A couple of the hands followed them unobtrusively, spreading out to flank them several hundred yards away. Jessica looked at the outriders and commented, "If we're going to have any privacy for our picnic, we're going to have to go back across the river."

"Any cowboy worth his salt's going to keep an eye on anybody visiting the home ranch. Man's got to know what's happening on the range he's responsible for."

"Oh, I don't mind," Jessica said. "I know they're doing their job."

Stark mulled over her comment about having some privacy for their picnic. He wondered what she had in mind.

As it turned out, a picnic was all Jessica had in mind, which was fine with Stark. He'd only known the lady a little over a day, after all. But he liked her and enjoyed her company, and he certainly enjoyed the fried chicken, baked potatoes, hard-boiled eggs, and buttermilk biscuits she had packed in those saddlebags. He wasn't sure how she'd managed to get so much food in them, but he was beginning to learn that Jessica Prentice was one talented woman. All in all, the afternoon they passed under some cottonwoods on the bank of a creek that ran into the Espantosa was one of the most pleasant Stark had spent in a long time.

It was early evening, barely past dusk, by the time they got back to Delgado. Stark had resisted the temptation to kiss her when they finished their picnic, but he wasn't sure he was strong enough to win that argument with himself again. Maybe when he left her at her house, she wouldn't mind a little peck on the cheek, or maybe a little more—

The yelling that came through the open door of the sheriff's office as Stark and Jessica rode past drove all thoughts of romance from his mind. He reined in abruptly when he recognized the angry voice of Malcolm Hawthorne. "What in blazes?" Stark muttered, then urged the Appaloosa toward the hitchrack. "Excuse me, Jessica, but I want to see what's going on."

"I'm coming with you," she said worriedly. "I hear Burton in there, too."

Stark recognized Garrison's voice now, as well as Sheriff Brewster's. It seemed as if everyone was talking at once. He swung down from the saddle, flipped the reins over the rail, and stepped up onto the boardwalk.

A shape came out of the shadows along the wall and moved into the rectangle of light that spilled through the door. The old desert rat called Nat stood there, his eyes shining with excitement. "Howdy, Judge," he greeted Stark. "Come to join the festivities, have you?"

"You know what's going on in there?" Stark asked.

Nat grinned broadly. "I seen the whole thing. Somebody just tried to ventilate that young Malcolm Hawthorne fella!"

Chapter Nine

Stark stared at the old man. "Tried to kill him, you mean?" he asked.

"Well, what else would I mean? Ventilate, ambush, bushwhack, dry-gulch—don't matter what you call it. Somebody came damned close to puttin' lead through that boy."

Stark realized it would take a while to get the whole story from Nat, so he pushed past him and strode into the sheriff's office. Phil Brewster was behind his desk, hands raised in the air as he motioned for Malcolm Hawthorne and Burton Garrison to calm down and be quiet. Brewster glanced over when Stark came into the room, and a look of relief washed over his face.

"Maybe you can make some sense of this, Judge," he said. "I sure as blazes can't!"

"It's simple," Malcolm said loudly. "Scott tried to kill me!"

"You don't know that for sure, Mal," Garrison put in, evidently playing the role of peacemaker. "You said you didn't see who took that shot at you."

"I didn't have to see him," snapped Malcolm. "I know it was Scott."

Stark looked at the young man and saw the outrage on his face. Malcolm was genuinely upset, but he seemed unhurt. "What happened?" Stark asked him. "Start at the beginning."

"All right," Malcolm said. "But I'm getting tired of telling this story when somebody ought to be out arresting that so-called brother of mine!"

"I've sent one of my deputies to fetch Scott," Brewster said. "He was here in town a little while ago."

"Well, he wasn't earlier," Malcolm snapped. He took a deep breath, then went on in a calmer tone, "I rode up onto our north range this afternoon, toward the hills. No particular reason, only taking a look around. That's where I ran into this old man."

He gestured toward Nat, who piped up, "That's right. I saw the whole thing!"

Stark wasn't getting to the bottom of things very fast, but he kept plugging away. "What happened then?" he asked Malcolm.

"Somebody took a shot at me from a ridge. The bullet plucked my hat right off my head! Damned near killed me!" As evidence, Malcolm held up a brown Stetson with a ragged tear in the crown that could indeed have been a bullet hole.

"Did you see who fired the shot?" asked Stark.

Malcolm shook his head. "He was hiding in some

scrub mesquite and got away down the other side of the ridge when he saw that he hadn't killed me. It had to be Scott. Everybody in town heard him swear yesterday that he wasn't going to let me inherit the ranch."

That was pretty much true, Stark thought. There were plenty of witnesses to Scott's threats against his brother. He asked Nat, "Is that the way you saw it?"

The old man nodded excitedly. "Darned right! Hell, that bushwhacker nearly got me, too! Why, I felt the wind of that bullet on my face as it come past me lickety-split—"

"Did *you* get a look at the gunman?" Stark broke in.

"Well . . . nope, I sure didn't. Heard his horse's hooves a-gallopin' away after he'd missed with that shot, but that's as close as either of us come to him."

Stark turned his attention back to Malcolm. "Have you seen your brother today, out at the ranch or anywhere else?" He didn't mention that he himself had paid a visit to the Boxed H. He hadn't seen any sign of Scott Hawthorne while he and Jessica were there, though.

"Scott packed his things and moved out yesterday," Malcolm said. "He hasn't been back since." The new owner of the Boxed H began to pace angrily back and forth. "He could have ridden back today, though, to take that shot at me."

"Does he own a rifle?"

"He does. A Stevens Crack Shot. Not much of a rifle for heavy use, but Scott never shot it often. Deadly enough, though." He held up his hat again, this time with a finger stuck through the hole in the crown.

Jessica had listened to the questioning in silence so far, but now she spoke up. "Do you really think your brother is capable of trying to kill you, Mr. Hawthorne? I mean, a fistfight is one thing, but an attempt at cold-blooded murder . . . ?"

Malcolm's face was bleak as he slowly shook his head. "I tell you, Miss Prentice, before this week I wouldn't have thought Scott had the guts for it, but now . . . All I can tell you is that I saw the hate in his eyes yesterday, and I reckon he could have pulled the trigger if he thought he had me in his sights!"

"That's a damned lie!" a new voice said harshly from the doorway.

Everyone swung around sharply, including Stark, whose hand went instinctively to the butt of his LeMat revolver. Scott Hawthorne appeared to be unarmed, however, as he strode into the office, followed by one of Brewster's deputies. He fixed a cold glare on his brother and went on, "I didn't try to kill anybody. I'm not sure it wouldn't be a good idea, though."

"Here now!" exclaimed Brewster. "I won't have talk like that in my office. Scott, somebody tried to bushwhack your brother this afternoon. He's got a witness and everything, and he claims the bushwhacker was you. What do you have to say about that?"

"What I've already said—that it's a damned lie! I've been right here in Delgado all day."

"Can you prove that?" Stark asked.

Scott looked at him. "Well, I think so. I took a room in the hotel, and I ate breakfast late in the dining room. Plenty of people saw me there. After that, I went over to the Red Horse and sat in on a poker game most of the afternoon. I went back to the hotel for dinner, then to the Red Horse again for a little faro. That's where I was when this gentleman came looking for me." He jerked a thumb over his shoulder at the deputy standing behind him.

Stark considered what he'd heard, then said, "Sounds like a solid alibi, all right. I reckon you won't mind if Sheriff Brewster goes over to the hotel and the saloon and asks some questions?"

Scott's shoulders lifted in a nonchalant shrug. "He can ask anything he wants to. I've told you the truth." His voice sharpened as he went on, "Mal's made up this story about an ambush to get everybody on his side. First he fakes that will, and now he's trying to get everybody thinking I'm some sort of crazy killer!"

"There's nothing fake about that will," Malcolm insisted hotly. "And somebody *did* shoot at me! This old man was there. He knows it happened."

Scott looked at Nat and sneered. "Some old desert rat. You could probably give him a bottle of whiskey and he'd say anything you wanted him to."

"Now hold on there one second, sonny!" Nat said. "I was tellin' the truth. Somebody tried to bushwhack this other young feller, like he said." He tugged on his beard. "However, was somebody to offer me a little drink, I don't suppose I'd turn him down. . . ."

"Time enough for that later," Stark said. He frowned at Scott and continued, "That alibi of yours sounds so good it could have been planned that way. How about that gent Cahoon? Do you know where *he's* been today?"

Scott flushed. "That's Cahoon's business, not mine. I'm not his keeper."

"I thought he was working for you."

"He's just a friend of mine," Scott said lamely, but no one in the room seemed to believe him.

"So you don't know where he was this afternoon?"

"As a matter of fact, I haven't seen him since last night. I assume he's still around town, but you couldn't prove it by me."

Stark nodded again. "All right. I suppose we'll have to take your word for it."

Malcolm's eyes widened. "Take his word for it? My God, Judge, if he didn't pull the trigger himself, his man Cahoon must have! You can see that, can't you?"

"I don't see anything that'll stand up as proof in a court of law," Stark replied sharply, "and that's what I'm concerned with here." He turned to the local lawman. "Sheriff, I'd check out Scott Hawthorne's story if I were you, and find out more about Cahoon. That seems to be about all you can do for the time being."

"I already wired Austin about Cahoon. There's nothing we didn't already know about him. But I'll ask around more and see what I can find out," Brewster said grimly. He eyed Malcolm and Scott. "I sure wish you boys'd decide to get along. Your daddy was my friend for a lot of years, and I got no wish to see either one of you in jail—or in a coffin!"

"I haven't done anything wrong," Malcolm said stubbornly.

"Well, neither have I," insisted Scott. "I'm going to find a way to get my share of the ranch back, if not the whole thing, but I'm going to do it legally."

"Hah! He says that after he's brought in a gunman to kill me!" Malcolm swung around, fists clenched in rage, to face his brother. "Well, if you can hire a gunslinger to fight your battles for you, so can I. You'd better watch your back from here on out, brother."

"Damn it, shut that talk up!" Brewster exploded.

The Hawthorne Legacy

Scott turned pale but didn't lose his composure. "I'm tired of all these threats. Scott, you go on back to the hotel and stay there. Mal, you'd best ride out while you can and head back to the ranch." He motioned for his deputy to accompany Scott to the hotel.

Grudgingly, still glowering at each other, the Hawthorne brothers left the sheriff's office. When they were gone, Brewster heaved a long sigh and said, "They're like a couple of old billy goats buttin' heads. I've never seen the like between brothers."

"Well, maybe it'll be quiet tonight," Stark said. "We can hope so, anyway."

Burton Garrison asked, "Who do you think shot at Malcolm, Judge Stark?"

"No way of knowing. Could have been Cahoon. He might have told Scott to stay in town and show himself around to be in the clear if anything happened to his brother. If it was Cahoon, I'm surprised he stopped with one shot."

"Perhaps some of the Boxed H riders were nearby and frightened him off," Jessica suggested. "I don't see why anyone else would have a reason to take a shot at Malcolm. It had to be Cahoon, but there's no way to prove it."

"And now Mal's talkin' about bringin' in a gunman of his own," Brewster said glumly. He looked at Stark. "If you ain't got any pressin' business elsewhere, Judge, I'd be much obliged if you'd stay here in Delgado for a spell. I've kept the peace, broke up a passel of saloon fights, and dabbed my loop on plenty of rustlers, but something like this Hawthorne business is more'n I know how to handle!"

Stark could hear the frustration in the old lawman's

voice. "I reckon I can play out a few more hands in this game," he told Brewster. "Wouldn't mind seeing how it all comes out."

"I'm afraid someone's going to be killed," Garrison predicted bleakly. "Unless those young men come to their senses, that is."

Stark knew that was a strong possibility, but he kept that pessimistic view to himself. Instead he turned to Jessica and said, "We had a mighty nice day. Sorry it had to end like this."

"That's all right," she assured him. "I'm an attorney, remember, so I know about the press of legal business."

"Well, I appreciate it. I'll escort you home—"

"That won't be necessary. I'm sure Burton won't mind seeing me home." She smiled to take any sting out of the words. "You and Sheriff Brewster may want to talk."

It wouldn't hurt if he and the sheriff made a few plans in case things got worse, Stark realized. Jessica seemed to be thinking a little more clearly than he was. "All right," he nodded. "If it's no problem for Mr. Garrison—"

"Oh, no problem, I assure you, Judge," Garrison said. "Jessica and I have business matters of our own to discuss. Something's been bothering me about this entire matter."

Stark knew that feeling. He said his good-nights to the two attorneys. Garrison offered Jessica his arm, and they left the office together.

When they were gone, Stark looked over at the somewhat disreputable sofa where Nat had parked himself. "You're still here?" he asked the old man.

The Hawthorne Legacy

"Nobody told me to leave," Nat replied. "Besides, I like seein' what's goin' on. I done told you, I came to the big city for some excitement." He chuckled. "Didn't figger to get shot at."

"I've been meaning to ask you—what were you doing on the Boxed H, anyway?"

"Wanted to have a look at the place, see what all the ruckus was about. Looks like a mighty nice spread, from what I saw of it 'fore that bushwhacker took a shot at the boy and he dragged me into town to back up his story."

"Wish you'd gotten a look at whoever fired the shot," Stark commented as he hung up his hat.

"Well, *I* sure as hell don't!" Nat declared emphatically. "If I'd seen the varmint, then he'd have a reason to try to kill *me*! I plan on stayin' out o' the line of fire from now on."

"Sounds like a good idea," Stark agreed. "The rest of us may not be able to, though."

"Well, that's a plumb shame." Nat tugged at his beard. "I disremember who it was, what with so many folks talkin', but somebody said somethin' a while ago about a drink...."

Sheriff Brewster pulled open a desk drawer and reached inside for a bottle. He said, "The way things are goin', that's the best idea I've heard all night."

Chapter Ten

Despite Stark's fears, the night passed without any further disturbances. Malcolm Hawthorne evidently returned to the Boxed H after leaving the sheriff's office, and Brewster's deputy reported the next morning that Scott had gone back to the Red Horse Saloon and spent the rest of the evening drinking and gambling at the faro table.

There was no railroad line through Delgado, but the telegraph wire had reached the settlement a few years earlier. On the morning following the attempt on Malcolm's life, Stark went to the telegraph office after breakfast and sent a wire to the Justice Department in Washington, explaining that the Hawthorne case had turned out to be more complicated than he had expected and that he would be remaining in Delgado a few days longer. Within the hour he had received a reply from an assistant attorney general reminding him that he was

The Hawthorne Legacy

due in El Paso in ten days to conduct hearings on a border dispute. As long as he arrived in time for those hearings, the Justice Department had no problem with his staying in Delgado for the time being.

With that chore taken care of, Stark went to the law office and found it empty. A note on the locked door explained that Jessica and Garrison had gone to the southern part of the county on business and would be back that evening. Stark looked up from the note to see Phil Brewster strolling down the boardwalk toward him, and he raised a hand in greeting.

"Do they have to go out of town like this often?" Stark asked as he indicated the note.

"Pretty regular. You got to remember, Judge, Burt and Miss Prentice are the only real attorneys we got in these parts. They handle legal chores for folks all over the county, and it ain't unusual for 'em to take off in Burt's buggy to visit their clients who don't live in town."

"Well, that makes sense. I was hoping to talk to them again about this Hawthorne mess, though."

Brewster grinned. "And maybe take Miss Jessica on another picnic?" he asked slyly.

Stark grimaced, then laughed and shook his head. "I reckon in a small town like this, most people don't have any secrets, do they?"

"Oh, you'd be surprised. There's plenty of gossip, right enough, but I suppose if folks tried real hard they could keep their business to themselves. Most don't bother tryin', though."

"Well, there's nothing going on between Jessica and me except maybe friendship and a common interest in the legal profession."

Brewster nodded solemnly. "That's what I figured."

Stark resisted the urge to take a poke at the lawman. Instead he accompanied Brewster on his rounds; then both of them went back to the sheriff's office. Stark spent the morning there, listening to Brewster's stories of the county's early days, when Delgado was merely a wide place in the road, the Comanches and Apaches were still a near-constant threat, and Emmitt Hawthorne, Wade Winthrop, and Brewster himself, among many others, brought civilization to this part of West Texas. Stark had come along in time to take part in the last of the Indian wars himself, and he had seen plenty of lawlessness as a shotgun guard, so he had some yarns of his own to swap with the sheriff. All in all, it was a pleasant morning. Not as pleasant as if he'd spent it with Jessica, he thought, but enjoyable nevertheless.

That afternoon he stopped by the Delgado General Store and waited until Todd Summers had finished taking care of a customer before extending a hand. "Don't think we've been formally introduced. I'm Earl Stark."

Summers gripped his hand firmly and smiled. "I know who you are, of course, Judge, but I'm glad to meet you. What can I do for you?"

"I wondered if you'd heard anything from the Boxed H today. I know that you and Miss Hawthorne are engaged to be married."

"Yes, but I'm not sure how soon the wedding will take place." Summers's earnest, handsome face turned solemn. "Lorna is still pretty upset about her father's death, naturally, and this trouble between her brothers, well . . ." He shook his head. "I think it's bothered her more than anything else. But to answer your question, Your Honor, I haven't talked to Lorna or anyone else from the Boxed H since yesterday afternoon. I heard about what happened to Malcolm. It seems that everyone in town is talking about that bushwhacking."

"Do you think Scott Hawthorne could have been responsible for it?" Stark asked. Summers knew all the players involved in this drama as well as anyone, and Stark was interested in his opinion.

For a moment Summers didn't answer. Then he said reluctantly, "Scott and I have always gotten along all right. I didn't have any problems with either of Lorna's brothers. So I hate to say anything against Scott *or* Malcolm. . . ."

Stark remained silent and let Summers work through the dilemma himself.

"I think it's possible," Summers resumed after a moment's hesitation. "Finding out that his father left the ranch to Mal did something to Scott, drove the wedge between them even deeper. I've heard that Scott has an alibi for the time of the shooting, but that his hired gunman doesn't. As far as I know, nobody's seen this Cahoon around town since day before yesterday. He could've tried to kill Malcolm, acting on Scott's orders." Summers put his palms on the counter and sighed heavily. "This is a terrible thing, and I shouldn't be talking this way."

"All you did was answer the question. I asked it. And for what it's worth, you're not the only one who feels that way. I reckon Cahoon's the most likely suspect, and a man like that doesn't try to bushwhack somebody unless he's being paid to do it."

Summers glanced around the store and lowered his

voice to ask, "I've heard that Malcolm threatened to hire a gunman of his own. Is that true, Judge?"

"He made the threat," Stark replied. "Whether he'll go through with it or not is anybody's guess."

"I hope he doesn't," Summers said fervently. "And I hope Scott gets rid of that man Cahoon. Delgado doesn't need this trouble, and neither does Lorna. It's tearing her apart."

Stark felt a surge of sympathy for the young woman. Summers was probably right about her emotional state. He thought about calling Malcolm and Scott together and trying one more time to talk some sense into their heads. He doubted it would do much good, but he could try.

"Thanks for your time," he told Summers. "I'll do what I can to keep things from getting worse." His eye fell on a large glass jar sitting a few feet away on the counter. "Say, are those jawbreakers?"

"Sure are."

Stark grinned. "Give me a bagful. Haven't had a good jawbreaker in a coon's age."

Summers scooped the candy into a paper sack and said, "That'll be a nickel." Stark paid him, took the sack, waved, and went to the front door of the store.

He paused before he stepped out onto the boardwalk and slipped a round jawbreaker from the sack. Wouldn't do for a judge, a dignified individual such as himself, to be seen walking down the street eating candy. But surely one wouldn't hurt.

Stark popped the jawbreaker into his mouth, stuck the bag containing the rest into his jacket pocket, and went out of the store. As long as he didn't have to talk to anybody for a while, he'd be all right.

The simple pleasures were always the best. That was God's truth.

He went by the law office later in the afternoon, but Jessica and Garrison still hadn't returned from their trip. Brewster invited him to supper at a chili parlor on one of the side streets, and Stark had to admit the sheriff's choice was a good one. The place served a Texas red that brought tears to Stark's eyes and made him gulp gratefully from the large mug of beer that came with it. The chili was followed by pecan pralines that were soft and sweet. Stark rubbed his belly when he was finished and wondered if he could unobtrusively loosen his belt a notch.

"Think I'll take a turn around the town," Brewster said. "Want to come along?"

Stark shook his head. "Thanks for the invitation, but I reckon I'll go on back to the hotel. I brought the briefs with me for those hearings I'm supposed to conduct in El Paso, so I'd better study up on 'em a mite."

Brewster pushed back his chair and stood up. "I'll see you in the morning, then." He grunted. "A day without trouble. That's been mighty unusual around here lately. We could sure use some more of 'em."

The sheriff was right about that, Stark thought as he returned to the hotel. Maybe Scott Hawthorne had come to his senses. Maybe Malcolm was willing to forgive and forget about the ambush attempt. Maybe he'd get to spend a peaceful day or two with Jessica before he had to move on.

He should have known better. He'd been sitting on the bed in his room with his boots off and his tie undone, studying the briefs for the hearings for about half an hour, when a knock sounded on the door. Out of habit he had placed the coiled shell belt with the holstered LeMat on the table beside the bed, within easy reach, so he reached over and put his hand on the butt of the grapeshot revolver as he called, "Who is it?"

"Burton Garrison, Judge Stark. Can I speak with you for a few moments?"

"Sure, hang on." Stark swung his legs off the bed and stood up. He left the LeMat where it was and went to open the door.

Garrison was alone. "Thank you, Your Honor. I'll try not to take up too much of your time."

"Where's Jessica?" Stark asked. "And how did your trip go today?"

"What? Oh. I left Jessica at her house, and our business went just fine." Garrison seemed distracted, as if something was weighing heavily on his mind. Stark closed the door and turned to face him, and Garrison went on, "I'll get right to the point. I've been looking at that will of Emmitt Hawthorne's, and there's something about it that bothers me. Besides the terms, I mean. I'm still convinced that it would be unlike Emmitt to leave such a meager legacy to two of his children."

Stark frowned. "Are you saying you think the will's not legitimate?"

"Last night I compared the handwriting to some of the other documents I know Emmitt wrote, and I think it's possible the will is a forgery." Garrison took off his hat, pulled a handkerchief from his pocket, and used it to wipe sweat from his forehead. "It pains me tremendously to say that, because—"

The Hawthorne Legacy

The glass in one of the windows suddenly shattered, and the shade over it fluttered. Garrison's head jerked. His body stiffened as blood and bone fragments burst out the side of his skull. Stark heard the spent bullet thud against the wall on the far side of the room.

Then Stark was diving to the floor, his arm sweeping out as he plucked the LeMat from its holster on his way down. Garrison crumpled like a marionette with its strings cut and lay at the foot of the bed, muscles still twitching in grim defiance of the death that had already claimed their owner.

Stark rolled over and scuttled around the end of the bed, one foot sliding a little in the pool of blood already forming under the murdered lawyer's head. Another bullet smacked through the window, and more broken glass sprayed into the room. Stark tried to avoid the sharp slivers as he reached out with his free hand, caught the cord on the bottom of the shade, and gave it a jerk. The shade rolled up with a rattle.

A third shot rang out just as Stark lifted his head above the sill. The bullet kicked splinters from the window frame and made him duck back, but he'd seen what he needed to see. The muzzle flash had come from the second floor of the building directly across the street. The bottom floor was a hardware store, Stark recalled, but he didn't know what was on the second floor—other than a murdering bushwhacker.

He thrust the six-and-a-half-inch barrel of the revolver over the sill and eared back the pivoting hammer, which was set for firing the .42 caliber cartridges in the cylinder rather than the buckshot shell in the center chamber. He squeezed off three shots as fast as he could cock and fire, aiming them at the window where the assassin's rifle had blazed. He had no way of knowing if he had hit anything, but no more shots came his way in return. His ears rang from the deafening blasts in the small room.

Stark twisted his head and looked at Burton Garrison. The lawyer's eyes were open but glassy. The first bullet had bored right through his brain, killing him instantly, seconds before he could say anything more about his suspicions of the will that had given Malcolm Hawthorne the Boxed H.

"Damn!" Stark said fervently. He and Brewster never should have given voice to the hope that the trouble was over, because it obviously wasn't, not by a long shot. Stark wondered if Garrison had told anyone else about his suspicions, someone like—someone like his partner.

"Oh, Lord!" Stark breathed as the thought hit him, and the next instant he was scrambling to his feet and plunging toward the door of the room. If he was right, then someone else might be in danger.

Jessica.

Chapter Eleven

"Judge Stark!" the desk clerk shouted when Stark pounded through the hotel lobby in his stocking feet a minute later. "What's happening? I heard shots—"

Stark ignored the man and ran through the door onto the boardwalk. His pulse was hammering in his head. He had never taken kindly to being shot at, and on top of that he was outraged by Garrison's murder and afraid for Jessica's safety. He had to find out if any of his shots had hit that bushwhacker.

More gunfire suddenly erupted in the night, but this time Stark didn't hear any bullets whipping around him. The shots sounded as if they were coming from the alley that ran behind the buildings on the other side of the street. Stark hurried toward a dark, narrow passage that ran alongside the hardware store to the alley.

He veered from his course when he reached the far

side of the street and bounded onto the porch in front of the hardware store, flattening his back against the wall at the corner of the passageway. The shooting had ceased while he was running across the street, but the night was still full of sounds. Men were shouting questions, and dogs were barking. The gunfire had the whole town in an uproar, and several men were running toward the spot where Stark waited, converging to see what the commotion was about.

"Stay back!" he called to them, hating to give away his position but unwilling to see innocents blunder into the path of a stray bullet. He motioned the citizens away from the dark passage and then stiffened when he heard harsh breathing. Someone was coming from the alley behind the buildings.

Stark waited until the breathing and the footsteps that accompanied it were only a few yards away, then pivoted around the corner of the building and went to one knee, the LeMat held level in front of him.

"Hold it!" he ordered sharply. He pulled back the revolver's hammer. The distinctive metallic sound seemed loud in the close confines of the passage.

"Don't shoot, dadgum it!" a querulous voice responded from the shadows. "It's only me, old Nat!"

"Nat!" Stark exclaimed. "What the hell are you doing back there?"

"Tradin' shots with some skunk who tried to kill me!" the old man said. "Like to run over me, he did, then threw lead at me. I got off a couple o' shots, but I don't reckon I hit him. It was mighty dark back there for shootin'."

Now that he thought about it, Stark recalled that the shots he'd heard had sounded as if they were coming

The Hawthorne Legacy

from two different guns. That fact supported Nat's story. He took a few steps into the passageway and asked, "What happened to the gunman?"

"Ran off down the alley," Nat replied. "At least, that's what it sounded like. What's goin' on around here, Judge? Hell, a feller can't even take a little *paseo* without runnin' into trouble."

"No time to explain now," snapped Stark. He tightened his grip on the LeMat. "I'm going to take a look around back there. You go see if you can find Sheriff Brewster and tell him where I am and what I'm doing."

Nat nodded, a motion only faintly visible in the thick shadows of the passageway. "You be careful, hear? That feller's downright *mean*."

The man he was after was more than that, Stark thought. He was a killer. Stark walked softly down the passage toward the alley, his revolver held ready. He could hear the curious questions being asked by the townspeople as Nat emerged onto the street in search of Sheriff Brewster.

Stark reached the alley and stopped to listen intently. He didn't hear anything moving around in the darkness, but that could be deceptive. The killer could be waiting back there for him to step out.

He'd never been one to stand still for fear of drawing trouble, though. Taking a deep breath, he moved smoothly into the alley. He wished he had thought to grab his greener before running out of the hotel; in close, dark quarters like this, the scattergun was a formidable weapon.

But so was the LeMat. He clicked the setting on the hammer up so that it would strike the nipple at the top of the frame that fired the buckshot barrel.

Only trouble was, there was nobody to shoot at. No one fired at Stark, and a quick search of the alley convinced him the killer was gone. A few minutes later, light spilled down the passageway leading to the alley. Brewster appeared, carrying a bull's-eye lantern.

"Judge Stark!" the lawman called. In his other hand he gripped his pistol, ready to fire. "You back here?"

"Take it easy, Sheriff," Stark answered. "That bushwhacker's already taken off for the tall and uncut."

"What bushwhacker?" demanded Brewster. "That old fella called Nat told me some wild story about somebody tryin' to kill him, and the clerk over at the hotel's yellin' about somebody bein' dead up in one of the rooms."

"It's true," Stark said grimly as he came up to Brewster. "Burton Garrison was in my room talking to me when somebody opened fire on us through the window. Garrison was killed by the first shot."

"Burt Garrison—dead! Lord, it don't seem possible."

"It's all too possible," Stark said. "The killer took a couple of shots at me from the second floor over the hardware store, but he ran when I returned fire. He stumbled over Nat back here in the alley and tried to shoot him, too. Where *is* Nat?"

"Right here," the prospector said from the passageway as he came into the circle of lantern light. "You all right, Judge?"

"Fine," Stark said curtly. "What did you see back here, Nat?"

"Not much—a shape in the dark, runnin' at me and damn near runnin' over me. He came from the back o' the buildin' here."

The Hawthorne Legacy

Brewster lifted the lantern and angled it so that its glow washed over the rear wall of the hardware store. All three men could see the window standing open on the second floor, directly over a stack of crates that might have served as a makeshift staircase.

"Reckon that's how he got in and out," Brewster said.

"What's up there?" Stark asked.

"Nothing. That floor's vacant. Ted Boley, who owns the store, rents it out sometimes, but there's nobody livin' up there now."

Stark had seen all he needed to back here, and worry over Jessica was pressing on his mind again. He had already wasted more time than he liked to think about. He said, "I don't know if the killer was trying for me or Garrison. Garrison was telling me he had decided that will of Emmitt Hawthorne's could be a forgery, after all."

"What?" exclaimed Brewster. "A forgery?"

"That's right. He may have told Jessica about it, too, and if he did, she could be in danger. Do you know where she lives?"

Brewster nodded. "She's got a house on Crawford Street. We'd better get over there!"

Stark and Brewster hurried along the passage to the main street. Nat followed without being invited. Stark didn't mind; another gun might come in handy. He glanced back at the long-barreled weapon Nat carried and asked, "What kind of horse pistol is that?"

"This ol' hogleg? It's a Paterson Colt. Ain't you never seen one before?"

Stark grunted. "Didn't know there were any of those still around."

"Carried it for nigh onto forty years, and it ain't let me down yet."

"Well, keep it ready," Stark advised. "You may need it."

The townspeople called questions to the sheriff as the three men hurried down the street, but Brewster ignored them. He said to Stark, "If that will was a forgery, then Scott Hawthorne may've been right. Malcolm could've been tryin' to steal the ranch from him."

"We don't know that," Stark cautioned. "I want to get to Miss Prentice's house and find out what Garrison told her, if anything."

As they passed the law office, a thought struck Stark, and he motioned for Brewster and Nat to stop. It wasn't likely that Jessica would be returning to the office tonight, but it was possible.

"Nat, why don't you stay here, in case Miss Prentice comes by?" he suggested. "She won't know anything about Garrison being killed, and it's early enough in the evening that she might stop by here."

"Not likely," Brewster said, "but possible enough that we ought to take precautions, I suppose. No time to hunt up any of my deputies, so I reckon the job's yours if you want it, Nat."

"Sure, I can do that," the old prospector replied. "What do you want me to do if the lady shows up?"

"Sit tight," Stark told him. "Get her inside and guard the door. Better not light a lamp, either. The sheriff and I will be along directly if we don't find her at her house."

"Don't worry about a thing, gents." Nat took up position in front of the law office door, arms folded across his chest and chin lifted proudly.

The Hawthorne Legacy

Confident that Nat would stand guard there, Stark and Brewster headed toward Jessica's house, the sheriff leading the way. It was only a matter of minutes, but it seemed to Stark to be taking forever. As they hurried through the night, he thought about what Garrison had said just before he was murdered. If Emmitt Hawthorne's will was a fake, there was only one person who could logically be responsible—Malcolm Hawthorne. That was another reason for leaving Nat on guard at the law office: Garrison could have left behind documentation of his suspicions, as well as the will itself.

And if Malcolm was willing to resort to murder to cover his tracks, he wouldn't hesitate to break into the law office. Stark hoped Nat stayed alert.

Moments later Brewster said, "That's it," and pointed to a small adobe house behind a yard full of shrubs and climbing plants. A stone path led to the door of the house. The sheriff had started up that path when Stark stopped him with a hand on the arm.

"Let's take a look around back," he suggested in a low voice. He had spotted the warm yellow glow of lamplight in one of the windows, and everything looked normal, but he wanted to make sure no one was sneaking up behind the house.

"Good idea." Brewster blew out the bull's-eye lantern. No sense in making themselves targets.

Stark went first, wincing a little at the sharp prod of gravel through his socks. At least, he thought wryly, he could move more quietly this way than he could wearing his boots. He held the LeMat ready as he slipped around the corner of the yard and went along the short fence that bordered it. The cottonwoods growing there threw deep shadows that helped conceal the two men.

When he was even with the back of the house, movement caught Stark's eye. He stopped, squinted, and picked out a figure walking behind the building. He touched Brewster's arm again and pointed.

Brewster nodded and lifted his gun. Without warning he bellowed, "This is the law! Hold it right there, mister!"

The figure twisted sharply, and a tongue of flame geysered toward them. Stark heard the bullet whine past as Brewster and he instinctively split up. He braced himself and squeezed the trigger of the LeMat. The shotgun shell roared, sending a charge of buckshot across the yard. Brewster opened fire at the same time, his .45 blasting. The muzzle flashes threw a garish orange glare across the scene.

The light wasn't enough for Stark to get a good look at the skulker, however. The man fired a couple more shots, one of which chewed bark from the trunk of the cottonwood Stark was using for cover. Brewster had gone to one knee behind a bench covered with flower pots, and one of the pots exploded, showering the lawman with dirt. Whomever they had surprised in Jessica's backyard was a good shot.

Stark had no doubt this lurker was the same man who had killed Burton Garrison. The fact that they had caught up with him here was further proof that he had been after Garrison all along. He must have intended to kill both partners in the law practice.

Stark ducked around the tree and aimed a couple of shots toward where he had last seen the muzzle flashes. He wasn't surprised when he apparently didn't hit anyone. The killer was too slick to stay in one place. In fact, a second later Stark heard hoofbeats close by. The man must have had a horse waiting behind the house.

He was about to give chase, knowing it would probably be futile, when the back door of the house opened and Jessica Prentice called in a loud, frightened voice, "Who's out there? What's going on?"

Stark cursed under his breath and flung himself across the yard. If the killer heard Jessica's voice, he might try one more shot, and a hastily fired bullet could be as deadly as a deliberate one if the fates so decreed. Stark left his feet in a dive, and Jessica gasped at the sight of the bulky figure hurtling out of the darkness at her.

His arm went around her slender waist and pulled her back, away from the door. Both of them went down, Stark landing with a grunt, Jessica letting out a cry that was as much surprised as pained. Stark put his free hand on her shoulder and said urgently, "It's me—Earl! Stay down!" He twisted to cover the doorway with the LeMat. Outside, more shots blasted, but none of the bullets came through the door or struck the house.

"My God, Earl, what is this? What's all that shooting—"

Brewster's voice cut through Jessica's frantic questions. "You all right in there, Judge?" he called.

"We're fine," Stark called in return. "What about the bushwhacker?"

"Gone," Brewster said disgustedly. A moment later he appeared in the doorway and went on, "He got away on his horse. I tried a couple of last shots, but I don't reckon I hit him."

"Damn! He's lucky, I'll give him that."

Jessica was sitting up now. She looked at Stark and Brewster in desperate confusion and asked, "Who? Will one of you *please* tell me what's going on?"

Stark got to his feet, stuck the LeMat behind his belt, and held out his hand to her. She took it, and he pulled her upright. There was no easy way to tell her what had happened, so he said bluntly, "Somebody killed your partner a little while ago, Jessica. I reckon the murderer came here to finish the job."

Her fair skin lost all of its color. "Burton . . . dead?" she whispered. "He can't be."

"I'm sorry." Stark's voice was gentler now. "I was with him when it happened. He was telling me he thought that the Hawthorne will was a fake, after all. Did he say anything to you about it?"

Her chin was trembling, but she managed to shake her head. "He didn't say anything about it to me. I . . . I could tell that something was bothering him over the past couple of days, and I think he started to tell me something a time or two, but then he . . . he stopped. He said he wanted to be sure before he started accusing people."

"Like Mal Hawthorne, you mean," Brewster said grimly.

Jessica lifted her face to look at them. Her eyes were damp, but she was not so overwhelmed by the news of Garrison's death that she was unable to think. "It had to be Malcolm," she declared. "He was the one who profited by the will, and he was the only one who would lose so much that he might be willing to kill to keep his secret."

"Hate to think that of the youngster, but it looks that

way to me, too," Brewster agreed. "I reckon I'll be takin' a ride out to the Boxed H. Mal's got some mighty tall explainin' to do." He looked at Stark. "Want to go along, Judge?"

"Maybe I'd better stay here," Stark began, glancing at Jessica. It might not be safe to leave her alone.

"Please go with the sheriff, Earl," she said unexpectedly. "I'm sure I'll be all right. And I want you to make certain that justice is done . . . for Burton's sake."

"Well . . . all right," Stark said slowly. "I reckon Sheriff Brewster can leave a couple of men here to keep an eye on things and make sure the killer doesn't circle around to come after you again."

"Darned right I can," said Brewster. "I'll get some men and be right back. Pick you up here, Judge?"

"That's fine," Stark said. "Get my Appaloosa from the livery stable and bring him along."

Brewster nodded and departed hurriedly, reloading his pistol. Stark looked at Jessica. She seemed to be keeping a tight rein on her emotions, but beneath the surface he knew she was shocked and saddened by her partner's death.

"It seems like such a long time ago that you and I went on that picnic, Earl," she said.

"You're right—a lot's happened since then."

She put a hand on his arm. "You'll find whoever killed Burton, won't you? If it wasn't Malcolm Hawthorne, I mean."

"I'll find him," Stark vowed. "You've got my word on that."

Once again, he had a personal stake in finding a killer.

Chapter Twelve

Brewster came back about ten minutes later with not only several deputies in tow, but also the old prospector called Nat.

"Missed all the excitement," the old-timer groused. "When I heard the shootin' over this way, I knew it was you and the sheriff havin' all the fun, Judge."

"Not hardly." Stark grunted. "We're riding out to the Boxed H. You'd better get your mule if you want to go along."

"Got him right outside," Nat said cheerfully. He seemed to have recovered from his earlier encounter with the mysterious gunman.

Brewster posted two of his men outside Jessica's house with orders to stop anybody who tried to get in, by force if necessary. The other two deputies would accompany Stark, Nat, and Brewster on their visit to the Boxed H.

The Hawthorne Legacy

Before they left, Jessica touched Stark's arm. "Be careful, Earl," she said quietly. "Malcolm may have gone mad."

"Don't worry," Stark assured her. "I intend to take care of myself."

And he intended to take care of Malcolm Hawthorne, too, he added silently, if Malcolm was the one who had killed Garrison and tried to kill Jessica.

Brewster handed Stark his boots and gun belt as they went down the stone path to where the horses were waiting. "Figured you'd want these," the lawman said.

"Thanks." Stark strapped on the gun belt, then stopped at the end of the path and leaned against a tree long enough to pull on the boots. Then he stepped to the side of his Appaloosa and swung up into the saddle. The others mounted at the same time. They headed west out of Delgado at a fast trot, Stark and Brewster in the lead, Nat bringing up the rear behind the two deputies.

They had gone less than half a mile from town when Stark spotted a rider in front of them, headed in the same direction. Since it was highly unlikely the killer would be lollygagging around this close to Delgado, none of the posse members drew their weapons as they overtook the man. The rider reined in and hipped around in his saddle to look at them in surprise.

"Is that you, Sheriff?" he asked. Stark recognized Todd Summers's voice. "What's going on? Is something wrong?"

"Damn sure is," Brewster replied. "You on your way out to the Boxed H, Todd?"

"That's right. I'm running a little late, too. Lorna expected me for dinner, but I couldn't get away from the store." Summers studied the grim faces of the men surrounding him and frowned in concern. "Something really is wrong, isn't it?"

"Burton Garrison was killed a little while ago," Stark told him. "We figured the same gunman was going to try for Miss Prentice, but we spooked him and he ran."

"My God," Summers said in shocked, hushed tones. "I heard some gunfire, but I never expected . . . Is Miss Prentice all right?"

"Luckily, yes."

"What does this have to do with the Boxed H?" Summers asked. "Isn't that where you're going?"

Summers was an intelligent young man, and Stark could see that he was quickly putting things together. Stark said, "When Garrison was killed, he was telling me he suspected that the will Emmitt Hawthorne supposedly left was a fake, a forgery."

"A fake?" echoed Summers. "But Mr. Garrison himself examined the will at the hearing and said that it was in Emmitt's handwriting."

"I reckon he'd decided he was wrong. And I figure that's why he was killed."

"Wait a minute. If the will was a fake, then Malcolm . . . you think *Malcolm* killed Mr. Garrison?"

"Looks like it to us," Brewster said. "Since you're on your way to the ranch already, why don't you ride with us?"

"Of course," Summers muttered distractedly, obviously thrown for a loop by what he had just heard. Stark could understand that. Summers had been friendly with both Scott and Malcolm Hawthorne; they were going to be his brothers-in-law when he married Lorna. But now, Scott had evidently hired a gunman to kill Malcolm, and Malcolm was the most likely suspect in the murder of Burton Garrison, one of Delgado's leading citizens. It was enough to make any man's brain spin crazily.

The group of riders, now larger by one, pushed on. When they reached Espantosa Gorge, Brewster reined in and said, "Damn! I forgot they're still workin' on the bridge. I guess we'd better go around."

Stark edged the Appaloosa toward the partially completed span. "I had a good look at the bridge yesterday," he said. "We can cross all right as long as we're careful."

He sensed the other men looking dubiously at each other behind him, but he didn't turn back. The floor of the bridge was in place except for a few spots, none of which were wide enough so that a horse couldn't step over them. A misstep, though, could plunge a mount's leg through one of the openings, and then if the animal panicked and began to thrash around, it could easily throw its rider. With no railing on the south side, a man could fall off the bridge and plummet to the bottom of the gorge three hundred feet below. Those thoughts went through Stark's mind as he urged the Appaloosa across.

The big horse had been through worse than this. Stark gave the Appaloosa his head, and the horse picked his way carefully across the bridge, lifting his hooves over the open spaces and never shying away from them. The other horses in the group weren't so icy-nerved, however. They tossed their heads and snorted as their riders urged them forward. The posse crossed without mishap, but Brewster wasn't the only one mopping sweat off his forehead when they reached the western rim of the gorge.

"Well, I reckon that saved us some time," the sheriff admitted. "Cost me a few more white hairs, though."

They pushed on, and the lights of the Boxed H came into sight a little while later. But light carried a long way on these Texas plains at night, so it took over half an hour more to reach the ranch house. Several windows were lit up, and judging from the light coming from the bunkhouse, the crew hadn't turned in for the night, either.

Dogs came out to meet the visitors, yapping stridently to announce their presence. Several hands strode out of the bunkhouse, and Malcolm Hawthorne appeared on the veranda of the main house. He was carrying a Winchester; visitors after dark always prompted caution in this part of the country.

Stark wondered if he had some other reason for having the Winchester handy.

As the posse reined in, Malcolm tucked the long gun under his left arm and lifted his right hand in greeting. "Howdy, Sheriff," he called. "Is that Judge Stark with you? What brings you out this way at this time of night?"

Todd Summers edged his way to the front of the group and spoke before either Stark or Brewster could tell him to be quiet. "There was trouble in town, Mal," Summers said. "Burton Garrison was killed, and Sheriff Brewster and Judge Stark think you might have been involved. Is there any truth to that?"

Malcolm gaped at Summers, then turned his startled gaze to Stark and Brewster. "Garrison's dead?" he asked. "This is the first I've heard of it."

"I hope you're telling the truth," Summers said, a hard edge in his voice, "for Lorna's sake."

Stark leaned forward in the saddle. "Since Summers here came right out with it, you'd better tell us where you've been this evening, Hawthorne."

"Wait just a damned minute," Malcolm said angrily. "Why do you suspect me? I didn't have anything against Burt Garrison. He was the family lawyer, and he was my dad's friend. I wouldn't hurt him."

"Not even to keep him from telling anybody he'd discovered that the will is a forgery?" Stark shot back, stretching the truth just a little. Garrison hadn't said that the will was definitely a fake.

"That's a lie! No offense, Your Honor, but you're starting to sound like my brother, and Scott's crazy!"

"Maybe not," Brewster said. "If that will really is a fake, you got more reason than anybody else to try to keep folks from findin' out, Mal. I don't like to say that, boy, but it's the plain and simple truth. Now, where were you this evening?"

"I don't have to answer that," Malcolm said stubbornly, shifting the rifle slightly in his arm.

This could turn ugly in a hurry, Stark thought. By his very attitude, Malcolm was strengthening the case against him. If he lifted the barrel of that rifle a little more, somebody was liable to start shooting.

The screen door of the ranch house banged open, and Lorna Hawthorne cried, "Stop it! Stop it, all of you! Has everybody in this county lost their minds?"

Todd Summers was off his horse in an instant, vaulting onto the porch to grasp Lorna's shoulders and force her back toward the door, out of the line of fire should any shooting break out. Meanwhile, Malcolm was clutching his rifle even more tightly, and Brewster and his deputies had their hands on their guns. Some of the Boxed H crewmen were running over from the bunkhouse. If trouble started, Stark had no doubt they would take the side of their boss. Innocent men were likely to be killed here in a matter of moments unless somebody put a stop to it.

Stark reckoned it was up to him.

"Everybody hold on, blast it!" he bellowed. "Ease off on those trigger fingers! There's law and order here, by God!"

"You're not in court now, Judge," Malcolm bit off tersely. "You're on my land."

In a quieter tone, Stark said, "Put that rifle down, son. There's no need for any shooting. We just want to get to the bottom of this."

"You want to railroad me for a killing I didn't do, that's what you mean."

"If you're innocent, tell us where you've been tonight," Stark challenged.

Lorna pulled away from Summers. "He doesn't have to," she said. "I can tell you. He's been right here on the ranch all evening."

Stark leveled his gaze at her. "Are you sure that's true, Miss Hawthorne?"

"Of course I am. The crew all saw him at supper, and since then we've been going over the books together. Our cook brought coffee to us a couple of times, so she saw him, too."

"I could have told them all that, Lorna," Malcolm snapped.

"Then why didn't you?"

He shrugged. "I don't like people riding up to my house at night and asking a lot of damn fool questions."

The wheels of Stark's brain were clicking over rapidly. He hadn't expected Malcolm Hawthorne to have such a solid alibi for the time of Garrison's murder, but it seemed obvious now that he couldn't have pulled the trigger.

That didn't mean somebody acting on his behalf couldn't have done it, though.

"You hinted day before yesterday that you were going to hire a gunman of your own," Stark said to Malcolm. "The stage from San Antonio came in this afternoon, I recall. Anybody get off it that we should know about?"

Even in the poor light, Stark saw the flicker of apprehension in Malcolm's eyes. "That's none of your business—" he began.

"It *is* our business," Brewster insisted. "Answer the judge, Mal."

"All right," Malcolm said abruptly. "A new hand arrived, that's true, but that doesn't mean he had anything to do with Garrison's killing."

"Trot him out here," Brewster ordered.

For a moment Malcolm looked as if he was going to argue some more. Then he shrugged and turned to the cowboys who had come from the bunkhouse. "Have any of you seen Parker around?"

"He got back a little while ago, boss," one of them replied uncomfortably. "You want I should go fetch him?"

"Yeah," Malcolm said. "You do that." He stared defiantly at Stark, Brewster, and the others.

The punchers hurried off to the bunkhouse, and after a couple of minutes of awkward silence, they returned with another man accompanying them. The newcomer was dressed more flashily than most cowhands, in black pants, white shirt, fancy vest, and flat-crowned black hat. A black shell belt supporting two holstered, pearl-handled Colts was strapped around his lean waist. His features were narrow and pitted by some childhood disease, and although his face was carefully expressionless, it still communicated an air of arrogance as he nonchalantly studied the visitors.

"You wanted to see me, Mr. Hawthorne?" he asked in a quiet, controlled voice.

"That's right, Walt. These gents are from Delgado, and they seem to have the idea you might have shot a man there earlier this evening."

A faint smile touched the man's thin lips. "So there was a gunfight, was there?"

"Cold-blooded murder was more like it," Brewster said with a snort of contempt. "A man was dry-gulched."

The gunman shook his head. "I fight my fights out in the open. I've never ambushed anybody in my life."

"This is Walt Parker," Malcolm put in. "Maybe you've heard of him."

Stark had indeed heard of Walt Parker. The man was a notorious shootist, his gun for hire to whoever could pay the price. But Stark couldn't recall any stories about Parker being a back-shooter or a bushwhacker.

"I could tell you weren't a regular cowhand," Stark commented to the gunman, "not in that getup. Operate out of San Antonio, don't you?"

"I can be found there sometimes," Parker replied with a shrug.

"Where could you be found earlier this evening, about an hour ago, to be precise?"

Again Parker shrugged. "I was taking a look around

the ranch. I like to see where I'm going to be working."

"Taking a walk at night?" Stark sounded skeptical.

"I can see pretty well in the dark." Parker smiled. "Like a cat."

"Anybody with you?" Brewster asked.

"No. I prefer my own company most of the time."

Malcolm spoke up again. "This is ridiculous, Sheriff. You and the judge can't prove Parker was in town tonight, mainly because he wasn't. As for that will, I'll stand by it. I found it right where I said, there in Dad's desk."

"How did you come to look there right before going to the hearing?" asked Stark.

"I suggested that Mal take one last look around," Lorna put in. "Are you going to accuse *me* of hiding the will there, Judge Stark?"

Stark shook his head. "No, ma'am, I'm not. I don't see that you'd have anything to gain from doing that." Another question had occurred to him. How would Malcolm have found out in the first place that Garrison suspected the will was a forgery? He would have had to know that to come into town gunning for Garrison.

Stark kept that puzzle to himself. He felt frustration welling up inside him. This trip to the Boxed H had not only failed to produce any solid evidence against anyone, it had raised even more tough questions.

Malcolm said, "Look, it's obvious you're not going to find what you're looking for here. I'm sorry about Mr. Garrison, but no one on the Boxed H had anything to do with his death. It's getting late, so why don't you ride on back to Delgado?"

"Damn it, Mal—" Brewster broke off his angry response and drew a deep breath. "Reckon you're right, son. But if you *did* have anything to do with Burt Garrison's murder, then God help you when I find out about it." With that, he wheeled his horse around and said to the posse, "Let's go, boys."

Stark sat there a moment longer, studying the people gathered on the veranda—Malcolm, Lorna, and Todd Summers—and the man standing at the foot of the shallow steps, Walt Parker. Then Stark turned the Appaloosa and rode after the others.

"What do you think, Judge?" Brewster asked when Stark drew alongside him.

"I think we've got to keep digging," Stark replied. "The key to this whole mess is somewhere. All we've got to do is find it."

Nat put in, "That sounds about like lookin' for gold, Judge. Ain't always easy, and when you stumble onto somethin' that looks promisin', it turns out to be nothin' but fool's gold."

The old codger was right, Stark thought. There were flecks of what appeared to be truth scattered all through this affair, but they didn't add up to even a nugget of fact. He and Brewster would have to keep prospecting.

And hope they struck pay dirt before somebody else got killed.

Chapter Thirteen

Ben Whitehead was a sturdily built man of about forty. His broad shoulders, barrel chest, and strong, blunt-fingered hands bespoke a man who had done his share of hard work in his earlier years. These days, though, he wore a suit and sat behind a desk as the owner and president of the First State Bank of Delgado.

Whitehead looked up from the documents arranged on the desk in front of him and said, "I'm sorry, Judge. But as far as I can tell by comparing it to these other papers, this will is in Emmitt Hawthorne's writing."

"You're not an expert on handwriting, though, are you, Mr. Whitehead?" asked Stark.

"Of course not," the banker replied, a touch impatiently. "But I've got eyes, and I see pretty good, if I do say so myself. I don't know what Burt Garrison found to make him think otherwise, but to me this looks like Emmitt's hand."

"Thank you, Mr. Whitehead," Jessica said as she reached out to take the will and put it back in the leather case she carried. "We weren't trying to force you into any sort of decision. We wanted your honest opinion. We've also had the will examined by several other men with whom Mr. Hawthorne had dealings, such as Mayor Pike and Dr. Silcox."

Whitehead nodded. "If you don't mind my asking, what did they think of it?"

"Nobody's willing to say it could be a forgery," Stark admitted. "I've looked at it myself and compared it to other things Hawthorne wrote, and I've got to say . . . the blasted thing looks legitimate to me."

Whitehead spread his hands and said, "There you go. Have you considered the possibility, Judge, that that bushwhacker was after *you,* and poor Burt had the bad luck to be there at the wrong time?"

"Could be, but that makes even less sense. Nobody in Delgado has any reason to want to kill me. Scott Hawthorne doesn't like the decision I handed down in that hearing, but he's a lot madder at his brother than he is at me. And killing me wouldn't get him that ranch."

"I'm afraid none of it makes much sense," Jessica said wearily.

Stark glanced at her. Her face was pale and drawn. Only twelve hours had passed since Garrison's murder; the funeral was scheduled for that afternoon.

In the meantime, Jessica had wanted to try to get to the bottom of things, so Stark had gone along with her. They had spent the morning trying to find out if there was any truth to Garrison's suspicions concerning the will. So far they had run into a rock wall.

Jessica stood up. "Thank you for your time, Mr.

Whitehead. I suppose I'll see you at the funeral this afternoon."

"Of course." Whitehead reached across the desk to take her hand. "The bank will be closed this afternoon in honor of Burt. He was a fine man."

"Indeed he was." Jessica smiled faintly and turned to leave the banker's office. Stark walked beside her.

When they were on the boardwalk outside, he said, "I've heard there are experts who can tell whether or not a piece of writing was really written by a particular person. Maybe we could send the will to one of them. I can wire the Justice Department—"

Jessica was shaking her head. "That's a good idea, Earl, but it would take quite a bit of time. I'm not sure the county has that much time left, not with both Scott and Malcolm having hired guns on hand."

"Think they'll come to the funeral?" asked Stark.

She looked at him sharply. "My God, I hadn't thought of that. There could be trouble."

"If there is, Brewster and I will be there to put a stop to it," Stark declared. He was hoping they were both wrong. Surely Malcolm and Scott could put aside their differences long enough for Burton Garrison to be laid to rest with dignity.

Both Hawthorne brothers attended the funeral, but they sat on opposite sides of the church. Lorna, with Todd Summers in a sober black suit beside her, sat in the middle pew, directly behind Stark and Jessica Prentice. Jessica was pale in her mourning dress, and as Reverend King performed the service, Stark reached over and took her hand. She squeezed his fingers tightly and smiled a little.

Emmitt Hawthorne's memorial service had been held

before Stark got to Delgado, but Stark was certain that Garrison's funeral was equally well-attended. Practically the whole town turned out, as did many of the ranchers from elsewhere in the county. After the graveside rites on Delgado's windswept boot hill, Stark saw to it that Jessica was driven back to her house. Then he turned to the scattering of mourners who were still on hand, Scott and Malcolm among them.

He walked over to Scott, who was standing by himself, hat in hand. The two men exchanged curt nods, and Stark asked, "Seen much of that fella Cahoon lately?"

"He goes his own way and I go mine," Scott answered. "I'm not his keeper."

"I notice he didn't attend the funeral."

Scott shrugged. "He didn't know Burt Garrison. Guess he felt it wouldn't be proper."

Stark looked around. Malcolm and Lorna were standing together, several yards away, but although some of the Boxed H crew were on hand, there was no sign of Walt Parker, the gunman. That came as no surprise, either. The hired guns were avoiding the site of this temporary truce.

It was probably too much to hope that Cahoon and Parker would kill each other off and leave everyone else alone, Stark reflected wryly. They wouldn't go up against each other unless they were forced to.

"I've heard rumors that Garrison thought the will my brother claims to have found was a fake," Scott went on. "Is that true, Judge?"

"It's true," Stark told him. "No one's been able to substantiate that, though, and Malcolm's sticking by his story."

"Surely you can see he's lying. He's probably the

one who killed Garrison. Either that or he had it done."

Scott had to be aware of the visit Stark, Brewster, and the other possemen had paid to the Boxed H following Garrison's death. It was common knowledge around Delgado. Scott was prodding an open wound to see if he could make somebody holler, Stark thought.

"The whole thing's being looked into," Stark said. "You be sure you keep Cahoon on a tight leash until we get things settled."

Scott put his hat on. "Like I said, Judge, I'm not Cahoon's keeper." He turned and sauntered away, leaving Stark with a jaw tight with anger.

A moment later, Malcolm stalked past with a cold glance in Stark's direction. Neither of the Hawthorne brothers had much use for him now, it seemed. Lorna barely nodded as she and Todd Summers passed him. The storekeeper glanced back at Stark, lifted his eyebrows slightly, and gave a tiny shake of his head, as if to express his sympathy and to indicate that there was nothing he could do about the hostility the Hawthornes were directing Stark's way. Stark nodded his understanding.

Brewster came up and said, "Well, at least there wasn't any gunplay at the church or here in the cemetery. That's somethin' to be thankful for these days."

Stark nodded slowly. "Nothing's been solved. The trouble's only been postponed."

"How about comin' back to the office with me and havin' a drink?"

"Not much else we can do right now, is there?" Stark grunted.

Two days passed. The whole town seemed to be holding its breath. Stark wired the Justice Department, inquiring as to the location of the nearest handwriting expert, who turned out to be in New Orleans. It would take two weeks, at the very least, to send the will there with a sample of Emmitt Hawthorne's writing and get back an opinion as to its legitimacy. The will itself was still in the safe in the law office while Stark tried to figure out what to do next. Jessica was pretty much leaving it up to him, since he was the highest legal authority in this part of the country. That was a burden Stark had experienced before, and he felt its weight again now.

He was in Phil Brewster's office, drinking coffee and talking idly with the lawman, when both of them heard the sudden pounding of hooves in the street outside. Stark was sitting on the old sofa by the front window. He twisted his head to look out and saw Malcolm Hawthorne dismounting from a fine-looking chestnut gelding. Several Boxed H hands were with him.

"Trouble on the way," Stark said as he stood up. "It's Malcolm Hawthorne, and he looks ready to chew nails."

Brewster was on his feet, too, when Malcolm slapped the door open and stalked into the office, trailed by a couple of his punchers. "This makes twice, Sheriff!" he said without preamble. "Are you going to wait until he kills me before you do something about it?"

"Twice for what?" Brewster asked. "And I don't much appreciate you bustin' in here like this, Mal."

"Sorry," Malcolm said curtly. "But a man gets upset when people keep taking shots at him, even when they miss."

"Somebody ambushed you again?"

Malcolm turned to face Stark. "That's right, Judge.

This time they shot the horse right out from under me. I managed to crawl into a gully and get some cover, and then some of my hands came along and must've spooked the bushwhacker. He got away again, damn the luck. I wanted to bring him in and show you who's been trying to kill me. Had to be either Scott or that Cahoon."

"Cahoon was back in town last night," Brewster put in. "Saw him playin' poker in the Red Horse. Don't recall seein' him around today, though." The lawman rubbed his chin. "Haven't seen Scott, neither. I'll send somebody to look for him."

One of the cowboys with Malcolm spoke up. "Reckon that won't be necessary, Sheriff. Yonder he comes now, and it looks like he's bound for this office."

Stark tensed at that news. He looked out the window, following the cowhand's pointing finger, and saw Scott Hawthorne hurrying across the street toward Brewster's office. Scott looked like a young man with plenty on his mind, none of it good.

Malcolm swung around toward the door, his hand moving toward the six-gun holstered on his hip. The Boxed H cowboys looked nervously at one another. The Hawthorne brothers were about to confront each other again, and all hell might break loose.

To forestall that, Brewster stepped out quickly from behind his desk and barked, "You boys stand easy! I'll be damned if there's goin' to be any gunplay here in my office. I'll arrest the first man who even *touches* a gun butt!"

"Arrest my brother, Sheriff," Malcolm said. "That'll put an end to all the trouble."

Stark seriously doubted that, what with Cahoon and Parker still in the picture. But he didn't say anything as Scott jerked the door open and swept into the office. Scott looked furious about something, but he came to an abrupt halt when he saw Malcolm and the Boxed H hands standing there. A shadow of nervousness flickered across his face, and his hand darted inside his coat, no doubt reaching for a gun.

Stark didn't wait to find out. He stepped forward, his hand shooting out with surprising speed. His fingers closed over Scott's wrist. "Don't do it, son," he advised in a low voice. "I don't know what's going on, but you're outnumbered here—not to mention that the sheriff and I don't want any shooting."

"I was going to defend myself," Scott said raggedly. He lifted his free hand and pointed a shaking finger at Malcolm. "His gunman just tried to kill me."

"What are you talkin' about?" demanded Brewster. "We didn't hear no shots."

"It wasn't very loud. I think he muffled the blast somehow. All I know is that I was on my way back to the hotel from the Red Horse, and somebody took a shot at me from an alley. The bullet hit a parked wagon that I was passing. You can come see for yourself, damn it. I drew my own gun and turned around, but whoever had shot at me was gone by then."

Malcolm laughed humorlessly. "What a ridiculous story. He's making up this feeble yarn to excuse himself for trying to kill me."

"I don't want you dead, Mal," Scott sneered. "I want you off that ranch."

"Well, that's something you'll never get." Malcolm moved toward Scott, hands clenched into fists.

Stark moved between them. "Hold on, you two," he said sharply. "Let's go take a look at this wagon Scott says was hit by the bullet. Maybe that'll tell us something."

"Good idea," Brewster added. He had his hand on the butt of his revolver as he cleared the office and then led the group down the street. Stark and he made sure they stayed between Scott and Malcolm.

"There it is," Scott said a moment later, indicating a heavy ranch wagon parked alongside the boardwalk. "You can see on the sideboard where the bullet hit."

Stark looked at Brewster. "You know who this wagon belongs to?"

"Can't say as I do," the sheriff said, shaking his head. "But that don't really matter. I want to see if I can find that bullet."

He ran his fingers over the spot Scott had indicated in the thick sideboard. There was a hole there, all right. Brewster took a clasp knife from his pocket and opened it. After a minute or so of prying with the short blade, he worked loose a small chunk of lead.

"A mite smaller than a regular forty-four or forty-five slug," he said as he bounced the deadly pellet on his callused palm. "A thirty-eight, I'd say. What do you think, Judge?"

He handed the bullet to Stark, who took it and studied it for a moment before nodding. "I think it's a thirty-eight, too." He looked at Malcolm. "Seems to me those fancy pearl-handled guns Parker carries are Colt Lightnings. Those fire a thirty-eight, as I recall."

Malcolm frowned. "Parker carries Lightnings, all right, but that doesn't mean he took a shot at Scott. You heard Parker yourself; he's not a back-shooter."

"'Course," Brewster mused, "that means takin' the word of a hired gunman if you accept that."

"Good Lord!" Malcolm exclaimed. "If Parker fired at Scott, don't you think he would have *hit* him?"

"Same thing could be said of Cahoon," Stark pointed out. "You've accused the man twice of trying to bushwhack you. Cahoon's a professional, so there's a good chance *you* would be dead if he'd been the one doing the shooting."

"But if it's not Cahoon—" Malcolm began.

"And if it wasn't Parker—" Scott interrupted.

"Then who is it that's tryin' to kill you boys?" Brewster concluded, rubbing his jaw and frowning darkly.

Malcolm shook his head. "I don't believe it, not for a damned minute. I don't know what's going on, but I know Scott's behind it. He's your troublemaker, and I demand that you arrest him, Sheriff!"

"Well, I demand that you arrest Malcolm!" Scott shot back. "Or is he too important now that he's stolen the Boxed H from me? Maybe he's too big a man to arrest!"

Brewster stiffened. "You'd better watch that kind of talk, Scott. I uphold the law around here, and I'll arrest any man I catch breakin' it! Trouble is, there's no proof that either one of you is right about what's goin' on."

Stark said dryly, "Could be the only way we'll find out for sure is to wait around and see if you kill each other."

"I'm not waiting anymore," Malcolm snapped. He glared at Scott. "You'd better be armed the next time I

The Hawthorne Legacy

see you, because I'm liable to shoot first and not waste time asking questions!"

"That's fine with me," Scott grated, "because I may shoot first myself!"

"Dadblast it!" Brewster yelled in frustration. "I'm tired of you boys threatenin' each other like that! Mal, you take your hands and get out of town. Scott, you make yourself scarce. And if I see either of them hired guns in town, I'm goin' to arrest 'em on general principles! Now git, the both of you!"

Stark and Brewster stood beside the wagon, watching Scott and Malcolm go their separate ways. When Malcolm and the Boxed H punchers had disappeared down the road leading out of town, Brewster heaved a long sigh.

"Those boys both got so many burrs under their saddles they ain't seein' straight anymore. Somethin' mighty strange is goin' on around here."

Stark still had the spent bullet in his hand. He lifted it, holding it between thumb and forefinger, and nodded, deep in thought. Brewster was right; it was beginning to look as if something else might be involved here besides the natural rivalry between Malcolm and Scott over their father's legacy. But no matter what was causing it, the county was primed to explode into violence, and once that happened, there would be no turning back.

Time was slipping away, Stark realized, and every tick of the clock was bringing them all closer to catastrophe.

Chapter Fourteen

Stark was sitting in the chili parlor the next day, having lunch, when the old prospector called Nat came in and sat down across from him. Nat looked at Stark's bowl, which was heaped high with meat and beans and peppers—buttered corn bread on the side—and practically licked his lips. Stark chuckled and signaled for the waitress to bring over another bowl of red, along with a mug of beer.

"Thanks, Judge," Nat said. "That chili's mighty good eatin'."

"You're welcome. What've you been up to? Haven't seen you around for a couple of days."

"Oh, I been busy with this an' that," Nat said cryptically. "Heard that both o' them Hawthorne boys got shot at again yesterday."

Stark nodded, his good mood blunted a little by the reminder. "They blamed each other, of course, or rather their hired guns. But nobody was hurt, which was lucky."

But was it really luck? Stark had been pondering that very question this morning without coming up with a satisfactory answer.

Nat changed the subject by saying, "I don't reckon this is any of my business, Judge, but I noticed somethin' else that has to do with the Hawthorne family. Not that will and the inheritance ruckus."

Stark frowned. "What's that?"

"Did you know that Todd Summers feller has hisself a lady friend?"

Stark's eyes widened in surprise, but before he could ask Nat what he meant, the waitress arrived with his chili, corn bread, and mug of beer. Nat grinned widely as the food was set in front of him.

"Thanky kindly for this grub, Judge," he said. "My funds are startin' to run a mite low."

Stark waved off his thanks as Nat crumbled the corn bread into the chili and dug in with the big spoon the waitress had brought. When Nat had swallowed a couple of bites, Stark leaned forward and asked in a low voice, "What did you mean by that, Nat? Todd Summers is engaged to marry Lorna Hawthorne."

"Sure, I know that. But that don't mean he ain't havin' a little fun somewheres else."

Stark's frown deepened. "How in blazes do you know about this?"

"Oh, I get around. Nobody pays much attention to an old geezer like me, but I pay attention, yes, sir, I do. I see things—like Summers sneakin' off from his store to meet some other woman."

"Where?" Stark asked sharply. He liked Lorna Hawthorne and felt sorry for her already because she had tried to keep the peace between her brothers and failed. She didn't need any more heartbreak in her life. It was hard to believe Todd Summers could be unfaithful; he seemed like an upstanding young man with plenty of genuine affection for Lorna.

Nat shook his head in reply to Stark's question. "I ain't sure yet where they meet, but I saw him slippin' up the street the other evenin' with a woman, and it weren't that Hawthorne gal."

"Could you see who she was?"

"Nope. She had on a hat and a veil, and it was pretty late, besides. No moon. All I could tell for sure was that she was a she."

Stark grimaced and took a healthy swallow of his beer. That sounded like mighty flimsy evidence that Summers was carrying on with another woman. She could have been a late customer Summers was walking home after closing the store. For that matter, Nat could have been wrong about the whole thing, and Summers's companion might not have even been a woman. Still, it was enough of a possibility to be worrisome.

As if he didn't have enough on his mind already, Stark thought. Now he was getting involved in the personal lives of the people mixed up in the legal tangle he had come to Delgado to straighten out.

The best thing to do, he decided, would be to put this concern to rest, one way or the other. To Nat he said, "How would you feel about doing a little chore for me?"

"Why, sure, Your Honor, I'd be glad to. What is it you need?"

Glancing around to make sure that no one in the chili

parlor was eavesdropping, Stark said quietly, "I want you to keep an eye on Todd Summers for me. If he *is* seeing another woman, I want to know about it."

Nat grinned. "Didn't figure somethin' like that'd be in your, what you call it, jury's diction, Judge."

"You don't have to do it if you don't want to," Stark growled.

"Oh, I'll do it. To tell the truth, I'm a mite flattered you want me to help you out. And I like a little juicy gossip as much as the next feller. Don't get much of it out in the desert, you know. Gila monsters and sidewinders and coyotes just ain't very good comp'ny."

"Well, if you find out anything, you come and tell me," Stark said. "I'll make it worth your while."

"No need for that. Just buy me a bowl of this here chili and a drink ever' now and then, and that'll be fine."

Nat hungrily fell to, scooping up the chili and washing it down with beer. As for Stark, he had lost some of his appetite, and he finally pushed his bowl away unfinished, which was a rare event. Nat thanked him for the food, scraped his chair back, and left the chili parlor with a friendly wave. Stark returned it halfheartedly.

It might be a mistake for him to get involved, but he wasn't going to sit by and let Lorna Hawthorne be hurt, not if he could do anything about it. If Nat came up with proof that Todd Summers was seeing another woman, Stark intended to pay Summers a visit. Summers would have to either forget about the other woman or break off his engagement with Lorna. That was all there was to it.

As he mused over this new development, Stark found

himself wondering about Nat, too. The old desert rat had insisted all along that he was staying in Delgado for the excitement of what he considered a big city. But it occurred to Stark now that nearly every time something happened, Nat was in the vicinity. Burton Garrison's murderer, in fact, had run into the old man in the alley behind Boley's hardware store. At least that was what Nat said had happened.

Stark shook his head. He was under so much strain he was starting to suspect a harmless old codger like Nat. There probably wasn't a deceptive bone in the old man's body.

On the other hand . . . maybe, while Nat was keeping an eye on Summers, someone ought to be keeping an eye on Nat.

Evening had slipped down on Delgado once more. Stark and Brewster were in the sheriff's office, Scott Hawthorne was in the Red Horse playing poker and drinking and flirting with the percentage girls, and Malcolm and Lorna were evidently out at the Boxed H; no one had seen them in town all day. Walt Parker was probably on the ranch, too, sticking close to his boss, while the gunman Cahoon was visiting an establishment on the edge of town known as Miss Lucy's, where the working girls had already learned his habits and shuddered a little when they saw him stride into the red-velvet-decorated parlor.

As for Todd Summers, he was locking the front door of his emporium when he heard the soft scrape of a footstep on the boardwalk behind him.

"Sorry, we're closed," he said as he turned from the door to face what he took to be a late-arriving customer. He tensed a little when he saw the disreputable figure standing there, thumbs hooked casually behind the frayed piece of rope that served as a belt.

"Don't want to buy nothin'." Nat leaned over and spat into the street. "Thought we might have us a little talk, Mr. Summers."

"Do I know you?" Summers asked with a frown. "I'm sure I've seen you around town, but—"

"Name's Nat. I don't reckon we been formally introduced, but I know who *you* are, mister, that's for damn sure."

"Look, I have to be somewhere," Summers said with a trace of annoyance. "If there's something I can do for you, please tell me so I can get on about my business."

"Oh, you're a busy man, are you? Should'a figgered as much, a nice, successful young feller like you. Should'a knowed you'd be busy as all get out. You got this store to run, and you're plannin' on gettin' hitched to Miss Lorna Hawthorne, ain't you?"

"That's right." Summers sounded more impatient than ever now, but he was also starting to sound worried. He tried to brush off the old man by saying, "If you've got something to talk to me about, it'll have to wait until tomorrow. I've got to be going—"

"Not so fast," said Nat, and there was a hint of something in his voice, something that made Summers stiffen. "I know some things about you, Summers, things that maybe Miss Lorna would like to know, too. I could ride right out to the Boxed H and tell her."

Summers was positively pale now, his face a white blur in the shadows. He tried to brazen his way through by saying, "I don't know what you're talking about, old man, but you're starting to bother me. Now, if you don't move along, I'll have to call the sheriff—"

"You do that," Nat cut in smoothly. "You call the sheriff, and call Judge Stark, too, while you're at it. You can explain everything to them, 'fore you have to explain it to Miss Lorna."

"You're either insane or drunk," Summers said, his voice trembling a little from the strain of keeping it under control, "and I don't have time for this." He started to push past the old man.

Nat's hand shot out and closed over his arm, the gnarled fingers digging in with surprising strength. "You'd best make the time, Summers," he hissed. "If you don't want me carryin' tales, you'd best make it worth my while to keep my mouth shut."

"That . . . that's blackmail!"

"I don't know the fancy word for it, but I know you'd be a damned fool not to play along with me, son. Miss Lorna's beautiful, and she might be rich one o' these days. Play your cards right and you ain't got a thing to worry about."

Beads of sweat had popped out on Summers's forehead. He asked in a voice like the croak of a frog, "Wha—what do you want?"

"I ain't decided yet," Nat replied smugly. "But I'll be thinkin' about it, and I'll let you know. Till then, you go on doin' what you been doin', but remember . . . somebody might be watchin'."

With that, Nat released the storekeeper's arm and turned, sliding away in the shadows and vanishing down a nearby alley. Summers stood there shaken, breathing almost as hard as if he'd just run a long distance.

The Hawthorne Legacy

The old son of a bitch! The man had his nerve, coming to him with that not-so-subtle blackmail attempt! Something would have to be done about him, Summers thought as his fear faded somewhat and was replaced by anger. Nat needed to learn to keep his nose out of things that didn't concern him. He had no business prying into the affairs of other people.

But if Nat would blackmail *him,* Summers suddenly realized, he might not be above approaching other victims, too. He wished he could be sure how much Nat knew about certain people and events in Delgado.

But if nothing else was a certainty, Summers knew that one way or another, Nat would have to be dealt with—and soon.

Chapter Fifteen

Stark and Brewster were standing on the boardwalk in front of the sheriff's office the next morning, Brewster puffing on his pipe, when the strangers rode into Delgado.

Brewster's teeth clamped down harder on the stem of the pipe, and he touched Stark's arm to get his attention. With a slight nod he indicated the six men who were reining in their horses in front of the hotel.

Right away, Stark didn't like the looks of them. They wore dusters, which wasn't unusual in this part of the country, but the long coats were pushed back to give the men easy access to the revolvers holstered on their hips. Their clothes were covered with trail dust, indicating a long ride, and under the pulled-down brims of their hats their features were hard and beard-stubbled. Stark had seen their like many times before, sometimes in the makeshift courtrooms where he held most of his trials, and before that over the twin barrels of his greener as he blasted to hell any desperadoes foolish enough to hold up a coach on which Big Earl was riding shotgun.

They were hardcases, pure and simple, and their presence here in Delgado couldn't mean anything but trouble.

"If they were goin' into the bank instead of the hotel, I'd be grabbin' a scattergun and yellin' for my deputies," Brewster commented worriedly. "What do you reckon they're doin' here?"

Stark shook his head. "Don't know, but I don't much like it. We don't need more trouble. I'll go give a listen."

"I'll come with you," offered Brewster.

"No, I'd better go alone. The sight of a badge might make them closemouthed."

Brewster didn't argue. Stark walked across the street to the hotel. All six men had gone inside after tying their horses at the rail, and as he entered the lobby he saw them standing in front of the desk talking to a nervous-looking clerk. Stark heard the clerk say, "—would check the Red Horse Saloon if I was you, gents. I'm afraid I don't know Mr. Cahoon personally, but surely someone at the Red Horse could tell you where to find him."

"What about this fella Hawthorne?" one of the strangers asked.

"Mr. Scott Hawthorne, ah, has a room here, but he's not in at the moment. You could likely find him at the Red Horse, too."

"Thanks," the spokesman said curtly. The group swung toward the hotel's entrance.

By this time, Stark had set himself down in one of the wing chairs that were scattered around the lobby. He was sitting next to a potted plant, and he picked up a copy of the Delgado *Courier* as the hardcases walked out. Although he seemed to be paying no attention to them, they were all he was thinking about at that moment. He was so preoccupied, in fact, that he was lucky to get the newspaper right side up when he lifted it in front of his face.

The six hardcases were pards of Cahoon—fellow gunmen, more than likely. He had probably summoned them to Delgado, and Stark could see only one reason for such a summons. Scott Hawthorne had to be getting ready for some sort of move against the Boxed H, a move that required more than half a dozen hired killers.

Stark didn't like it at all.

He tossed the paper aside, left the hotel, and crossed the street to Brewster's office. He glanced at the Red Horse in time to see the last of the strangers vanishing through the batwings. He had no doubt they would find either Scott Hawthorne or Cahoon—or both of them—there.

Brewster was waiting anxiously. "Find out anything?" he asked.

"More than I wanted to," Stark replied grimly. "I think Cahoon sent for them."

The veteran lawman knew what that meant as well as Stark did. "Aw, no," Brewster said. "It's gonna be a shootin' war after all, ain't it?"

"Starting to look like it."

"You reckon I'd better send a wire to Austin and ask for a company of Rangers?"

"It wouldn't hurt, but it'll take a while for them to get here. If anything happens in the meantime, we'll have to deal with it as best we can."

The strangers did indeed find Cahoon in the Red Horse. Stark went down to the saloon a few minutes later to check on them and saw them sitting around a large table at the rear of the long, narrow room, talking with both Cahoon and Scott Hawthorne. Scott seemed a little uneasy, Stark thought, as if he hadn't expected the newcomers to look quite as menacing as they did. But the men were passing around bottles and seemed to have settled in where they were. Either Stark or one of Brewster's deputies kept an eye on the place all afternoon, and the hardcases didn't leave.

What with worrying about this new development, Stark didn't think about Nat and his story concerning Todd Summers until that evening. Then he recalled that he had set Nat to watching Summers and tried to remember if he had seen the old man around anywhere during the day. But Nat hadn't shown his face even once, which was unusual.

About an hour after nightfall, though, after supper in the hotel dining room, Stark was strolling along one side of Delgado's main street when he saw Nat on the other side. He lifted a hand and called out to him.

Nat stopped and waited while Stark crossed the street. The old man looked rather nervous and fidgety. Stark nodded a greeting and asked, "Something wrong, Nat?"

"Nope, nothin' wrong," Nat answered quickly. "Why would somethin' be wrong?"

Stark laughed without much humor. "Well, damned

near everything else has gotten bollixed up since I came to Delgado. I just thought maybe you were having problems, too. Did you find out anything more about Summers?"

Nat rubbed his bearded jaw. "Well . . ." He cast a glance at the building in front of which they stood, and Stark noticed for the first time that it was a cantina.

"Come on inside," he said. "We'll sit down and have a talk. *And* a drink."

Nat grinned, looking more like himself again. "Sounds like a right fine idea," he said.

Stark waited until they were ensconced at a small table in a corner of the cantina before bringing up Summers again. A pretty young Mexican waitress in a brilliant red skirt and a white blouse scooped daringly low over her impressive bosom had brought Stark a *cerveza* and Nat a glass of *pulque*. Stark sipped the beer while Nat downed the fiery liquor. "What about Summers?" Stark prodded gently.

Nat shook his head. "I ain't found out a thing, Judge." A shamefaced expression appeared on his grizzled features. "I was afraid to tell you for fear that you'd be disappointed."

"And that I wouldn't buy you a drink."

"Well . . . that, too, I reckon."

"Don't worry, Nat. I don't expect miracles."

"That's good, 'cause I got to thinkin' that I might've steered you wrong, Judge."

Stark leaned forward over the table. "What do you mean by that?"

Nat hesitated, then said, "Could be I was wrong about Summers. I don't want to get a feller in trouble when he ain't really done nothin'."

Stark bit back his irritation. "Are you saying you imagined the whole thing?" he asked. "Or did you make it up to cadge a few drinks and some chili out of me?"

"Make it up?" Nat repeated indignantly. "No, sir, I didn't make it up. I saw what I saw, dadgum it! But maybe I leaped to a conclusion or two—"

"And maybe you didn't," Stark said. "Look, Nat, if you don't want anything more to do with this, that's fine. I'll confront Summers myself and find out what's going on. And don't worry, I'll still stand you a drink now and then while I'm in Delgado."

Nat shook his head vigorously. "No, sir, Judge, you ain't got to do that. I'll hold up my end of the bargain. I just don't want you gettin' mad at me if it don't come to nothin'."

"You tell me the truth about whatever you find out about Summers, Nat. That's all I ask," Stark assured him.

"Sure, I can do that." He held up his empty glass and raised his eyebrows inquisitively, and Stark signaled the waitress to bring him another drink.

When Nat had tossed back the second shot of *pulque* and Stark had drained the rest of the beer, they stood up to leave. Stark tossed a greenback on the table to cover the drinks. A Mexican was strumming on a guitar, and he began to sing as Stark and Nat went out the open door into the night. The soft, fluid music followed them as Stark said his farewells and turned to head back to the hotel.

He had taken only a couple of steps when shots rang out behind him.

He reacted instinctively, whirling around and sweeping aside the tails of his coat so that he could reach the LeMat. He saw Nat crumpling to the ground a few yards away. Flame lanced from a shadowed alley between the cantina and the next building, and Nat's falling body jerked under the impact of another bullet.

Stark leapt toward the old man and heard a slug whip past his own head. Smoothly he palmed out the LeMat and brought it up, switching the hammer from the .42 cartridges to the shotgun shell as he cocked the weapon. It boomed and bucked heavily against his palm as he squeezed off the buckshot round.

Somebody in the alley screamed, but another shot blasted, the bullet kicking up dirt a couple of feet to Stark's right as he went down on one knee beside Nat's body. He calculated there were at least two bushwhackers in the alley. Rage welled up inside him. There had been too damned much sneaking around in this case, too many shots from ambush, too much lying and plotting. He was determined these would-be killers wouldn't get away.

He thumbed the LeMat's hammer back to its regular firing position and threw a couple of shots into the mouth of the alley. More noise and flame spat at him. He felt something pluck at the sleeve of his coat as he fired again and again.

Stark sent five rounds into the alley, then stopped firing. No more blasts came from the shadows. He heard running footsteps behind him and was about to spin around to confront a possible new threat when he heard Brewster's voice call, "Take it easy, Judge! It's me!"

"Careful, Phil!" Stark said. "They opened up on us from that alley, and they could still be in there playing possum."

He heard the ominous double click of a shotgun being cocked. "If they are, they'll damn sure regret it," Brewster said.

Stark came to his feet as Brewster moved up cautiously beside him. Together they approached the alley, their weapons held ready. When they got closer, Stark heard a peculiar bubbling, rasping sound and realized it was the breathing of a badly wounded man. It was followed by a hollow rattle—a man's final breath departing his body.

"Anybody else in there?" Brewster demanded.

Silence was the only answer.

The alley where the bushwhackers had lain in wait was quiet, but the rest of Delgado wasn't. Men were shouting and dogs were barking, and several men were running toward the scene of the shooting. Brewster looked around and saw one of his deputies approaching with a lantern. "Bring that light over here," he called to the man.

Stark wasn't surprised by what the glow of the lantern revealed. Two men lay sprawled on the dusty floor of the alley. One of them had been hit at least twice, high on the chest, just below the throat. He had to have been the one who died as Stark and Brewster approached the alley, because the other man had been killed instantly. This man was lying on his back and had a single hole in his forehead, above the right eye. Stark shuddered to think what damage the bullet had done to the back of his head as it emerged.

"Mighty good shootin'," Brewster commented. "You know either of these fellas you killed, Judge?"

Stark studied their faces, which were frozen in grimaces of shock and agony. Both men were complete strangers to him.

"Never saw them before," he replied with a shake

of his head. "From the way they're dressed, I'd say they're drifters, maybe outlaws, but they're not part of the bunch that rode in this morning."

"Where'd they come from, then? And why were they shootin' at you?"

"Maybe they were shooting at Nat," Stark said. He turned and walked quickly toward the old prospector, who still lay where he had fallen in the street. Someone was kneeling next to him. As Brewster's deputy trailed along with the lantern, Stark recognized the man tending to Nat as Dr. Hardy Silcox. One of the bystanders must have summoned him.

"How is he, Doc?" Stark asked as he holstered the LeMat and bent over the old man.

Silcox glanced up. "I think he'll live. He's lost some blood, but the wounds appear worse than they actually are. If I can get some help, I'll take him over to my office and give him a thorough examination."

Brewster "volunteered" several men to carry Nat to Silcox's office. Once the old prospector was stretched out on the cloth-covered table in the examining room, Silcox cut away his faded long underwear and began treating the two bullet wounds, one in Nat's upper left arm, the other a fairly deep crease in his right side. Silcox had chased everyone out of the room except Stark and Brewster.

"He'll be all right," Silcox assured them a few minutes later. "The wound in his arm is a clean one, and the bullet missed the bone. The one in his side is nothing to worry about, either, except for the possibility of blood poisoning, which is always a risk with any gunshot wound. But I feel confident that he'll recover." Silcox looked down at Nat, who was starting to moan and move his head from side to side as consciousness seeped back into his brain. The doctor continued, "I'd say he's a very lucky man."

"Lucky?" Nat repeated in a weak voice without opening his eyes. "D-damn! Ain't that just . . . just like a sawbones?"

Silcox chuckled. "You're alive, my friend—thanks to Judge Stark. From what I hear, he saved your life."

Nat's eyes flickered open, and he gazed up at Stark as the judge moved over beside the table. "Is . . . is that true, Judge?"

"Hell, I didn't know if they were shooting at you or me," Stark told him. "Somebody starts slinging lead around me, I shoot back. Reckon it's an old habit too hard to break."

"Sawbones is right," Nat whispered. "Lucky for me you was there."

Stark glanced at Silcox. "Can I talk to him for a few more minutes?"

"Let me clean up these wounds and bandage them first."

As Stark stepped to one side to wait, Brewster said to him, "I'm goin' back down to the cantina to make sure them bodies are carted off to the undertaker's. And I'll ask around to see if anybody knows who they were."

"I wouldn't count on that," Stark said.

"I ain't, but I reckon I at least got to try." With a shrug Brewster turned and left.

A few minutes later, Silcox finished bandaging the wounds. "All right, Judge Stark," he said. "Only don't wear him out. He's going to need some rest."

"Don't worry, Doc. I only need a few questions answered. And if you don't mind, we could use a little privacy."

Silcox looked a little puzzled by the request, but he nodded. "Certainly."

When the doctor was gone, Stark stepped over to the table again. Nat looked up at him apprehensively. "What is it you want to know, Judge? There ain't much I can tell you. All I know is somebody started shootin' and I got in the way. I reckon they was after you—"

"No," Stark said flatly. "I thought about that, too, but they had a clear shot at me from where they were. They were after *you,* Nat, despite what I said earlier while the sheriff was still here. Got any idea why somebody would want to kill you?"

Nat licked his lips and didn't answer for a moment, then said, "Well . . . maybe they thought I'd made a gold strike whilst I was prospectin' and figured on robbin' me. That could've been it."

Stark shook his head. "I don't think so. Like the doctor said, Nat, I saved your life, and I'm going to collect on that debt right now."

"I . . . I don't know what you mean—"

"You've been hanging around Delgado for days, and every time something happens, you're somewhere close by. You come to me with that story about Todd Summers and some mysterious woman, and then a day later somebody's trying to kill you." Stark's voice grew harsher as he went on. "I'm not the smartest hombre in the world, Nat, but I'm starting to get the idea there's more to you than just an old desert rat. I want the truth, and you might as well give it to me." He reached out, snagged a chair, and drew it over beside the examining table to sit down. His voice was hard as stone as he said, "I'm not going to budge until I know it all, Nat. The whole story."

Chapter Sixteen

When Stark stepped out onto the porch of the doctor's office twenty minutes later, his bearded jaw was taut with anger. Nat had played him for a sucker, that much was certain, and Stark was sure the old man hadn't told him the whole truth even now.

The truth, the whole truth, and nothing but the truth . . . Evidently Nat had none too solid a grasp of that particular concept.

The old man had admitted that he'd approached Todd Summers and hinted that he would reveal Summers's indiscretions to Lorna Hawthorne if the storekeeper wasn't willing to pay to keep him quiet. Nat insisted that he hadn't made any monetary demands—yet.

"Why didn't you go to Summers first, instead of telling me what you saw?" Stark had asked.

"Figured I'd better lay the groundwork, 'stead of

springin' the whole thing on you too quick," replied Nat as he lay on the examining table, pale from nervousness and loss of blood. "I wanted to have things ready, in case Summers told me to go to hell."

"Then you would have given me all the facts, instead of playing me along?"

"Yeah," Nat mumbled. "I would've told you about the house."

The house was an isolated cabin on the outskirts of Delgado, Nat had gone on to explain, and that was where he had really seen Todd Summers and the unidentified woman with him. "I reckon that's where they get together," Nat had speculated. "There ain't nothin' close by around the place, and if he didn't go there 'cept after dark, nobody'd know."

"Except an old busybody like you who wouldn't hesitate to blackmail him with the information."

"Damn it, I been ploddin' through the wilderness for nigh onto forty years, lookin' for gold and silver, and I ain't never found enough to do more'n keep me in beans and sourdough." Nat's eyes flashed with indignation. "I figured it was time I cashed in after all these years."

Stark hadn't wasted any breath arguing with him. He said flatly, "Tell me where to find the house."

Nat had hesitated, then given him the directions.

Now Stark stood on the porch, frowning and wondering if there was any more to the story than Nat had already admitted. Nat had insisted that his proximity to the various ambush attempts was sheer coincidence, and nothing Stark said could shake him from that position. Either he was telling the truth—or he had a damned good reason for being so stubborn.

The Hawthorne Legacy

The first thing Stark had to do was find out more about Todd Summers. It made sense that instead of paying blackmail money to Nat, Summers might have decided to invest in a couple of drifting hardcases who had no qualms about shooting an old man from ambush.

Dr. Silcox would be keeping a close eye on Nat, who would remain at the doctor's house while his wounds healed. Stark hoped that keeping Nat out of circulation for a while might help clear up some of the complications that had muddied this case. He left the doctor's office and strode toward the east end of town, not bothering to get his Appaloosa from the livery stable. His destination was within walking distance.

He didn't stop when he passed the sheriff's office, either; this was a chore he needed to handle by himself. He walked to the edge of town, where the road that led to San Antonio looped into Delgado from the south to avoid a small, flat-topped hill directly east of town. A narrow trail led off to the north, skirting the hill on that side; on the northern slope of the hill, according to Nat, was the adobe cabin where Todd Summers kept his rendezvous with his mistress. Stark couldn't see any lights out there, but that didn't mean anything. A man and woman sneaking around on the sly would be careful about things like that.

Stark walked along the moonlit trail until he neared the hill, and sure enough, there was the house. He had never noticed it before, which wasn't surprising; the adobe was the same color as the hillside behind it, and several scrubby mesquite trees around the building served to camouflage it further. As close to town as it was, the place was well hidden.

As Stark approached, his eyes searched for any sign that someone was there. He suddenly heard hoofbeats and the creaking of buggy wheels and hurriedly moved off the trail, into a clump of mesquite, hoping he wouldn't step on a rattlesnake in the darkness.

A buggy rolled past on the trail, heading toward town and moving briskly enough that Stark couldn't get a good look at the driver. He thought whoever was at the reins was wearing a veil, though, which would indicate a woman. He stayed where he was, and sure enough, a few minutes later a man rode past on horseback, going in the same direction.

He wasn't hurrying, and Stark was able to make out his features in the moonlight. The rider was Todd Summers.

"Damn," Stark breathed to himself. A part of him had hoped that Nat was wrong somehow, that maybe the old man had gotten confused about what was really going on. But he felt certain now that Summers was involved with the woman who had driven past in the buggy. There was nothing on this trail but the little adobe house, and no reason—except the obvious one—for Summers to have met the woman out here.

Stark had to decide what to do next. Confront Summers? Try to find out if the storekeeper had hired those two bushwhackers to kill Nat? Summers was a smooth one, and he wouldn't be easily rattled or spooked into a confession, if he was guilty. But it might be easier if Stark had enough ammunition to hit him with. Stark now knew where Summers was carrying on with the woman; if he knew her identity, too, that might be enough to throw Summers for a loop and get him to talking.

The Hawthorne Legacy

He started back into town, headed for the county tax assessor and collector's office. Nobody knew as much about what went on in a county as the fella in charge of the taxes.

A light caught his eye as he walked quickly down the main street. It came from the law office that was now occupied by Jessica Prentice alone. Stark veered in that direction. With everything that had been going on, he and Jessica hadn't had another chance to get together for several days. They had seen each other only in passing. He had been busy keeping up with the Hawthorne mess, and Jessica had had her hands full trying to handle all the work that had landed squarely on her shoulders following Burton Garrison's death.

She might be able to give him a hand with his research, however, so Stark seized the excuse to see her again. He knocked lightly on the door of the law office and heard her call, "Who is it?"

"It's Earl Stark."

A couple of seconds later, he heard the lock click over, and the door opened. He was glad Jessica was being cautious. There hadn't been any further attempts on her life, but it never hurt to be careful.

She greeted him with a warm smile. "Hello, Earl. Come in."

Stark stepped into the office, and she closed the door behind him. She was wearing a long black skirt and a lacy white blouse that Stark thought looked mighty pretty on her. He would have said as much, but his mind was still full of what he had discovered about Todd Summers, the mystery woman, the little adobe hideaway, and old Nat.

"What brings you here tonight?" Jessica asked. "Not

that I mind the interruption." She gestured at the desk covered with documents lying in haphazard piles. "I've been wading through this paperwork for so long I feel like I'll never get finished with it."

"Well, I've got some paperwork of my own to do, and I was hoping maybe you could give me a hand," Stark said. "I hate to bother you with it, but—"

"Nonsense. I'm glad to do whatever I can. Is this something to do with the Hawthorne case?"

"It has to do with the Hawthornes, but only indirectly. You don't happen to know who owns that house out there beside the hill east of town, do you?"

Jessica frowned. "What house? I didn't know there was anything out there around Blevins Hill."

"Is that what it's called? I didn't know. Anyway, there's a little adobe out there, and I need to know who it belongs to, if anybody."

"Well, we can certainly find out. The county tax records should show who owns the land."

"That was my thought," Stark said. "You know the tax assessor?"

"Edward Sprague. Burton and I frequently had dealings with him."

"Reckon he'd mind if we rousted him out and got him to let us look through his records?"

"No need to do that. Sheriff Brewster has a key to the office, since it's right next door to his. You and I can find what we need without disturbing Edward."

That idea appealed to Stark. He had been prepared to bring the tax assessor in on this, but the fewer people who knew what he was investigating, the better. "That's a fine idea. Can we go over there now?"

"Of course. As I said, I'm grateful for the interruption. Let me get my jacket."

The Hawthorne Legacy

Stark waited while she took the garment from a hook and slipped it on. She locked the door of the law office behind them, took Stark's arm, and walked beside him across the street and down a block to the sheriff's office. As they went in, Brewster looked up from his desk and grunted, "No luck on them two dead gents. Nobody I talked to had ever seen 'em before."

"Dead men?" Jessica said in surprise, arching her eyebrows.

"A couple of hombres wounded that old prospector, Nat, a little while ago," Stark explained. "I was close by, so I got mixed up in the fracas. They wound up dead. I'm surprised you didn't hear the shooting."

"I'm not," Jessica said. "That's how wrapped up I've been, trying to deal with all those documents. When I'm really concentrating on my work you could set off a cannon next to me and I might not notice it."

"I don't reckon I'll test that little theory," Stark said dryly. "Sheriff, Miss Prentice says you have a key to the county offices next door."

"That's right," Brewster said. "You need to get in there?"

"I'd like to take a look at a map of the county and some of the tax records," Stark told him. "You can come along if you want, make sure I don't bother anything."

Jessica added, "I thought perhaps we could avoid disturbing Mr. Sprague, Sheriff."

"Sure, no need to do that." Brewster rummaged around in the middle drawer of his desk for a moment, then came up with a long, heavy key. "This is it, I think. I'll come with you and unlock the door. Not that I don't trust you, Judge, but I'm curious what you're up to."

Stark grinned. "I'm not completely sure myself."

As they went next door, Brewster asked how Nat was doing, and Stark filled him in on the old man's condition without mentioning any of the things Nat had told him about Todd Summers. Brewster unlocked the door, went inside, and lit a lamp on the desk. Stark saw a big map of the county pinned to the wall behind the desk and knew that was where he needed to start.

"There," he said, resting a blunt finger on the northern slope of Blevins Hill. "I need to know who owns that land right there."

"That should be easy enough to determine," Jessica mused. "The survey records are in this cabinet over here."

As she riffled through the files, Sheriff Brewster turned to Stark and said, "Maybe it ain't none of my business, Judge, but you sure got me bumfuzzled with all this."

"I'm not trying to keep you in the dark deliberately, Phil," Stark told him honestly. "I'm not sure yet what I've got hold of, and I want to find out a little more before I do anything else."

Brewster nodded, but he didn't look happy. Stark liked the veteran lawman and wished he could answer his questions, but in a delicate matter like this, the fewer people who knew the whole story, the less likely it was that someone like Lorna Hawthorne would get hurt.

"Here's the survey that lists that property, Earl," Jessica said a few minutes later. "Now all I have to do is check it against the tax records. . . ."

Stark waited while she took a large document from one cabinet, carried it over to another cabinet, and began looking through the files there. She seemed to know exactly what she was doing, and Stark was glad he had recruited her for this effort. He could have rooted around in this office all night and maybe not found what he needed.

"Here," Jessica announced triumphantly in what seemed like no time at all. She brought a handful of documents to Edward Sprague's desk, spread them out in the light of the lamp, and rested a fingernail on one of them. "Here's the name of the person who owns that land."

Stark peered down at the paper and read the name. "Evelyn Rogers?" He looked up at Jessica and Brewster. "Either of you know somebody named Evelyn Rogers?"

Jessica shook her head blankly, and Brewster said, "Never heard of her. And I thought I knew everybody hereabouts."

"Let me check something else," Jessica said. She opened a large, thick book that lay on Sprague's desk and flipped through the pages, pausing after a moment to say, "According to this, Evelyn Rogers paid the taxes on that land for this year in cash. Before that, she also paid cash for the back taxes that were due on it, which is how she claimed ownership of it in the first place. The previous owner had defaulted on his taxes and the county took over the land as a result."

"When are the taxes due again?" Stark asked.

"Not for another five months."

"And neither one of you has ever heard of her?"

Stark's two companions shook their heads, but Brewster said, "This land you're talkin' about . . . has it got a little adobe cabin on it?"

"That's right," Stark replied.

"Shoot, I remember that place now. Ain't nobody lived out there for years. Nobody livin' there now, far as I know."

Maybe nobody was living there, Stark thought, but the place was sure getting some use anyway. He kept that to himself and said, "Would you mind asking around about this Rogers woman, Sheriff? Find out if anybody in town knows her."

"Sure, I can do that," Brewster said, a little testily. "Seems like you got enough on your plate with takin' on something else, though, Judge. No offense."

"None taken," Stark assured him. "Fact is, you're right."

Brewster held out the key to the office door. "Lock up when you're through here, if you don't mind," he said. "I'll be gettin' back to my own office now."

"Sure. Thanks, Sheriff."

Brewster nodded and went out. Stark gave a little shrug and turned to Jessica.

"I'm just as curious as the sheriff is," she told him with a smile. "And I should be a little put out with you, too. After all, if it wasn't for us, you wouldn't have found out what you wanted to know."

"That's true," Stark admitted. "Still, I reckon I better keep this to myself for now. I'm sorry, Jessica."

"Oh, I respect your decision, Earl. I'm sure you have a good reason for what you're doing." She came closer and put her hand on his arm. "I'm glad I could help."

She was only a few inches away, and her head was tilted back slightly so that she could look up at him. Stark didn't think about what he was doing. He kissed her.

Her lips were warm and soft and sweet-tasting, and

after a moment Stark put his arms around her. When the kiss was over, she whispered, "You'll have to leave Delgado soon, won't you?"

"Not until I'm finished here," Stark told her.

"Then I'll see you again."

"You can count on it," Stark said.

She slipped out of his embrace. "I've got to get back to work. As pleasant as this is, it doesn't take care of business."

"Nope," Stark agreed with a sigh. "And I reckon we've both got business to take care of." He offered her his arm. "I'll walk you back to your office, though."

"That's an offer I'll gladly accept."

They parted at Jessica's office, and Stark headed down the street to the hotel. He didn't feel like confronting Todd Summers tonight, but he thought he had enough evidence now to break through any defenses the storekeeper might try to put up. He had the name of Summers's lover, even though he didn't really know who the woman was.

But the more he pondered it, the more he thought that Brewster might have been right. Unless Summers was responsible for siccing those gunmen on old Nat, he hadn't done anything to break the law. A man's personal business was just that—personal. A judge had no right to go poking around in it.

Unless Summers had crossed the line into lawlessness by trying to have Nat killed—and damned near getting Stark killed in the process. If that was the case, then God have mercy on him, because Earl Stark sure as hell wouldn't.

Chapter Seventeen

Malcolm Hawthorne reined in at the top of the rise and pointed to the forty head of cattle strung out in the narrow valley below him. He and his companions had been searching for them all morning.

"Move them back down to the east pasture," Malcolm told the half-dozen ranch hands who had ridden with him into the foothills this morning. "I want 'em handier when it comes time for branding."

The cowboys started toward the cattle on horseback, moving slowly so as not to spook the stock. Walt Parker, sitting easily in his saddle beside Malcolm, said dryly, "You don't want me to help round up those strays, do you?"

Malcolm shot him a sharp glance. "That's not why I hired you, and you know it."

Parker chuckled humorlessly. "Sure, sure."

Swallowing his irritation, Malcolm swung his horse

around. He didn't like Parker, hadn't liked him the minute the man had arrived on the ranch several days earlier in response to the wire Malcolm had sent to San Antonio. Parker was arrogant, and he looked at Lorna in a way that made Malcolm's jaw clench. But the gunman was a necessary evil as long as Scott had that cold-blooded killer, Cahoon, working for him.

Parker looked around suddenly, as if something had alerted him. Malcolm hadn't seen or heard anything, but he supposed a man like Parker had to develop highly sensitive instincts if he wanted to live very long.

Parker pointed to a line of cedar trees back down the ridge. "Somebody's coming."

Eight riders emerged from the trees. Malcolm recognized one of them right away as his brother, Scott. Next to Scott was the rangy figure of Cahoon, and even at this distance Malcolm could tell that the other men were cut from the same cloth. Malcolm felt a finger of ice trail down his back. It was like watching a twister blowing straight at you.

He twisted his head around and shouted to the Boxed H hands who had started down the far side of the slope after the cattle. They reined in and looked back, and Malcolm motioned for them to return.

"Good thing you're bringing them back," Parker said in a low voice. "I can handle Cahoon, but not him *and* six others like him." He made a dry, rasping sound in his throat that reminded Malcolm for all the world of a diamondback rattler sliding over a rock in the hot sun. "Those boys of yours aren't going to be much use against men like that."

"There's eight of them and eight of us," Malcolm pointed out.

Parker shook his head. "Those odds only *sound* even."

Malcolm knew what he meant. The Boxed H riders were cowboys, young men who could handle themselves in a fight, but they weren't professionals. Cahoon and his men were.

Quietly Parker said, "As soon as I heard those boys rode into Delgado, I figured they'd get around to paying us a visit sooner or later."

"What should we do?" Malcolm asked, hating the feeling of helplessness stealing over him.

"They want to talk, we talk," shrugged Parker. "They want to fight, we fight. Somebody dies. Simple as that."

A shudder ran through Malcolm. It took a special kind of man to contemplate death—perhaps his own—so offhandedly. Malcolm would never be like that, never wanted to be like that.

But this ranch was his now, and he would fight for it if he had to.

Even to the point of killing your own brother? he suddenly asked himself.

There was no time to ponder that question. Scott and the others had reached the top of the rise and reined in. Some twenty feet separated the two groups of riders.

"We've come to settle things, Malcolm," Scott called.

"Everything's already settled," Malcolm replied. "You might as well turn around and ride back to town. And take your friends with you."

Scott glanced at Cahoon and the other gunmen. He seemed nervous, but Malcolm could understand that; he was pretty edgy himself.

"Look, I've been thinking about this," Scott said. "I don't guess I can blame you for faking that will—"

"It's not a fake, damn it!"

Scott shrugged. "Whatever. I reckon the Boxed H is worth it. But I can't let you get away with cutting me out of my share." He took a deep breath. "I swore I wouldn't settle for less than running the whole ranch, but this trouble between us has gone on long enough. I'm willing to work with you and share—"

"Watch it, boss!" Cahoon cried suddenly. His left arm shot out and shoved Scott out of the saddle, while his right hand swooped to his hip and brought up his Colt. "That ranny's going for a gun!"

"Wait!" Malcolm cried, but he was drowned out by the boom of Cahoon's gun.

One of the Boxed H punchers grunted under the impact of the bullet and went backward off his horse. The cowboy next to him yelled, "That son of a bitch shot Charley!" and clawed for his own pistol.

Walt Parker drew his twin Colt Lightnings with a speed that matched the name of the guns. But as they cracked, Cahoon shifted his horse aside so that Parker's slugs missed. Cahoon's men and the Boxed H riders were all jumping into the battle now. Guns blasted, filling the air with noise and powder smoke that stung the eyes and nose. Two more ranch hands slumped out of their saddles before Malcolm shouted, "Let's get out of here!"

His own gun was in his hand, and he snapped a wild shot at the knot of gunslingers working for his brother. Hatred for Scott welled up in Malcolm's throat like the taste of bile. That unholy devil had talked about a truce, lulling Malcolm and the others out of their wariness, then launched a murderous attack.

In the back of his mind Malcolm knew that wasn't exactly how it had happened, but there was no time to think about that now. Three Boxed H men were down, and more would die unless they found a place to fort up. The guns of Cahoon and the others were still blazing behind them as they galloped down the far side of the ridge into the little valley, their mounts at times barely able to stay upright at the breakneck speed their riders demanded.

Parker was racing his horse alongside Malcolm's. "Did you get any of them?" Malcolm yelled over the pounding hoofbeats.

"Don't think so," Parker called back. "Any cover around here?"

Suddenly Malcolm remembered an old line shack on the other side of the valley. It wasn't used much anymore, but it was sturdily built, and its thick walls would stop most bullets.

"Come on!" he called as he reached the bottom of the slope and put his horse into a dead run across the valley. "Follow me!"

Parker and the Boxed H men did just that. Their sudden flight had given them a short lead on their pursuers. Malcolm threw a glance over his shoulder and saw Cahoon and the others about fifty yards behind. That gap was too wide for effective shooting, especially with a pistol from the back of a running horse. There was still such a thing as blind luck, however, and as Malcolm watched in horror, one of his punchers threw up his hands with an anguished cry and slid out of the saddle. As the cowboy hit the ground and rolled over and over, Malcolm caught a glimpse of the dark bloodstain already spreading across the back of his shirt.

Then the swirling dust kicked up by the horses hid

that grisly sight, and Malcolm turned his attention back to his own survival. The line shack was in the trees on the far side of the valley, only about a quarter of a mile away. None of the Boxed H men, including Parker, were firing now. They were all concentrating on trying to outdistance Cahoon and the other gunmen.

Malcolm looked back one more time before he reached the line shack. He couldn't be sure, but he thought Scott was hanging back from the others slightly. Malcolm knew his brother; Scott really had no stomach for violence. Now that the bloodletting had begun, he would be content to stand back and wait until it was all over to reap the spoils. Malcolm's jaw tightened. At that instant he would have given about anything to have a clear shot at his brother.

They were almost at the shack now. Malcolm leaned forward to urge his horse on to greater speed, and as he did something slapped at the top of his left shoulder. He gasped in pain as the impact drove him even lower over the neck of the galloping chestnut stallion. His left arm went numb, and even though that was something of a relief, he knew he had been hit by one of those wild shots his pursuers were firing. The real pain would set in later, once the numbing shock wore off.

He drove that worry from his mind. He had to get himself and his men into that line shack if they were going to have any chance of coming out of this alive. With his good hand, which was also holding the reins, he pointed to the cabin and shouted, "Over there!"

All four men raced through the trees and flung themselves off their mounts as they reached the clearing around the shack. Malcolm staggered when his feet hit the ground, but one of his men caught his good arm and kept him from falling.

"Get him inside!" Parker rapped as he twisted around and palmed out his revolvers again. They began to crack in steady rhythm, one shot following another as fast he could pull the trigger. He lay down a withering hail of fire that made Cahoon and the others pull up and veer off as they reached the edge of the trees. Parker backed toward the open door of the cabin and was the last one through it, throwing himself to the side as rifles began to blast from the trees. Winchester rounds thudded into the logs of the door as it was slammed shut and latched behind him.

Malcolm was sitting on the dirt floor inside the hut, breathing heavily and trying to ignore the pain building in his left arm and shoulder. "We made it," he said. "We can hold them off from in here."

"Yeah, but for how long?" Parker asked bluntly. "We'll run out of shells after a while, and then all they'll have to do is rush us and wipe us out."

"We'll make them pay first for what they done, the bastards!" one of the cowhands said furiously. He had his rifle in his hands, and he knelt at one of the chinks between logs that had been left there deliberately when Emmitt Hawthorne built the line shack decades earlier. The cowboy slid the muzzle of his Winchester through the opening and began firing. The other cowhand looked for a hole of his own so that he could join his pard in returning the fire that raked the shack.

Parker's lips drew back from his teeth as he knelt beside Malcolm. "Yeah, we'll make 'em pay," he said bitterly, "but in the end we'll still be dead."

"I thought . . . I thought that was one of the risks of the job," Malcolm said.

Parker gave a hollow-sounding chuckle. "You're right. Might as well enjoy it while it lasts." He looked at the wound on Malcolm's shoulder and added, "You'll live, by the way. Probably hurts like hell, but that bullet only clipped you. Of course, the next one'll probably be fatal."

With that, he turned and scrambled across to the front wall of the shack, staying low in case any bullets penetrated the wall. He found a chink between the logs, eased the barrel of one of his Lightnings through it, and began squeezing off carefully measured shots.

Malcolm felt for his own gun and found it in his holster. He hadn't even realized he had jammed it back in. Now he drew it again and lifted it with a shaking hand as more waves of pain washed over him. He knew he probably wouldn't get a shot at Scott, but maybe he could save one bullet for Cahoon. That would be something, at least. . . .

He wished he'd had a chance to say good-bye to Lorna.

Scott Hawthorne flinched and fought the urge to put his hands over his head and hunker down even more as he knelt behind a tree trunk. He heard some of the bullets coming from the line shack thud into the wood above his head. The sound made his stomach clench in fear and frustration.

He had never intended for things to go this far, never! If only there were some way of communicating that to Malcolm and getting him to believe it . . . Sure, he had brought Cahoon and the other men with him, thinking that a show of force might make Malcolm more reasonable, but it hadn't worked out that way. One of the Boxed H men had reached for his gun—probably at some hidden signal from Malcolm—and everything had gone to hell after that.

Cahoon was crouched behind another tree about ten yards from where Scott knelt. The big gunman was wearing a grin, the first Scott had seen him display. Cahoon looked like a kid on the Fourth of July, reveling in the explosions, drinking in the acrid scent of gun smoke. Killing was obviously what the man lived for.

Maybe the Boxed H rider *hadn't* gone for his gun. Maybe Cahoon had gotten impatient for the shooting to start. It was a chilling thought, but one Scott couldn't ignore.

Cahoon worked for *him,* damn it, not the other way around. If Scott wanted to call this off, then, by God, he could call it off.

"Cahoon!" he called urgently, hoping the man could hear him over the continuing racket of the gunfire.

After squeezing off another shot toward the shack, Cahoon jerked his head toward Scott. "What is it?" he demanded impatiently.

"I . . . I want you to stop this!" Scott said, summoning up his courage. "I want you to call it off and stop shooting!"

Cahoon stared at him for a second as if he hadn't heard correctly. Then a curse burst from his thin-lipped mouth. "Call it off?" he repeated contemptuously. "Your brother's hit, maybe dyin'. This ranch is practically yours already. We ain't callin' *nothin'* off!"

Scott's eyes widened in horror. "Mal was wounded?"

"Damn right. I saw those cowboys drag him inside."

"Oh, my God," Scott breathed as he looked down at the ground. All the anger in him dissipated immediately. The bitter memories, the hurt feelings, the resentment he'd felt toward Malcolm—all of it was wiped away by the knowledge that his brother was hurt.

And it was his fault, Scott realized. All his fault—

"Cease fire!" he yelled abruptly. "Stop shooting, all of you!"

The other men ignored him, didn't even look around at him from their positions behind trees and rocks as they continued to pour rifle and pistol fire on the cabin.

Cahoon's face twisted in a snarl as he turned and darted across the open space between the trees. He dropped into a crouch next to Scott and hissed at him, "Those boys don't take orders from you. They do what *I* tell 'em, and I say it's time to put an end to this."

"But if Mal's hurt, I have to help him, get him to town and a doctor—"

"We're goin' to kill him if he's not already dead, you dumb son of a bitch!" Cahoon kept his anger in check with an effort and went on, "The only reason my pards came out here was the promise of a big payoff. That's the only reason I'm here, too. And there's not *goin'* to be a big payoff unless that brother of yours is dead! So shut up and keep your head down. You're worth too much to us to get your brains blowed out now!"

Cahoon turned back to the cabin and lifted his revolver. Before he could pull the trigger, though, Scott suddenly lunged forward and grabbed his arm, dragging it down. "No!" Scott cried. "I didn't want it to be like this!"

Cahoon cursed again and ripped his arm free from Scott's grip. He lashed out with the pistol, slapping the barrel against the side of Scott's head. Scott's hat flew off and he fell backward, stunned.

Muttering, Cahoon grasped one of Scott's ankles and pulled him behind the tree. Then he went back to firing at the line shack while Scott lay there moaning, only half-conscious.

Somehow it had all gone wrong, Scott thought with the small part of his brain that was still working. It had gone wrong, and there was no way to put it right again.

Charley Davenport hunched forward in the saddle, trying to hold his guts in with one hand while he guided the horse with the other. That was what it felt like, anyway. Ever since he had regained consciousness and seen the rest of the Boxed H hands riding off with the hired guns pursuing them, Charley had been trying desperately to hang on to his own life.

Not for himself, but for Malcolm Hawthorne and the Boxed H. Charley had managed to get to his feet somehow, and he had caught the dangling reins of his mount even as the horse shied away from the smell of the blood soaking Charley's midsection. As the gunfire faded in the distance, Charley had found the strength to pull himself up into the saddle and turn the horse toward Delgado. It would take at least an hour to reach town and summon help, and Charley didn't know if he had that long to live. But he wasn't going to die without trying. Charley Davenport rode for the brand, by God, and nobody had ever been able to say different.

Moaning, swaying in the saddle, the warm wetness spreading through him, Charley urged the horse forward and hung on for dear life.

Chapter Eighteen

Judge Earl Stark was frustrated. He had been trying all day to get Todd Summers alone so that he could broach the subject of Evelyn Rogers, the abandoned house at Blevins Hill, and a certain old prospector who had almost been killed the night before. But Summers's general mercantile had been so busy that Stark hadn't had the chance to approach him yet. He could have gone in and asked Summers for a private meeting, but that would have alerted the man that something was up. Stark didn't want to give him even that much warning.

He had gone by the doctor's house earlier to check on Nat and found the old man complaining that Silcox was making him stay in bed and rest. "Hell, I been hurt worse'n this when I cut myself shavin'," Nat had insisted, "back in the days when I still shaved."

Stark had advised the old-timer to follow the doctor's orders, then walked over to the law office. Jessica wasn't there, however, so he wound up in Phil Brewster's office that afternoon, mulling over what he had learned the night before. The sheriff seemed to have gotten over his irritation at Stark and was as friendly as ever.

Stark was about to pour some coffee for both of them when he heard the shouting in the street outside. Brewster heard it, too, and asked, "What in tarnation's goin' on out there?"

As he placed the coffeepot back on the stove, Stark leaned over, peered out the window, and saw a hunched-over figure on horseback surrounded by townspeople. "Looks like a man hurt, maybe shot," he told the sheriff. "We'd better go take a look."

They hurried outside and found a couple of bystanders trying to help the rider down from the horse. Stark saw the blood soaking the man's shirt and knew he'd been gutshot. A sour taste came up his throat. Somebody was yelling for the doctor, but Silcox wasn't going to be able to do any good. Nobody could now.

"Careful with him there," Brewster said sharply. "Why didn't you take him to Doc Silcox's place instead of bringin' him here?"

One of the townsmen looked up. "He wouldn't go to the doc's, Sheriff. Said he had to come here, and when we tried to get him off the horse, he like to rode over us."

The rider looked up, his face gray and haggard. His eyes didn't want to focus. He croaked, "Sh-sheriff?"

"Right here, son," Brewster said as he moved to the man's side. "Ain't you Charley Davenport, from the Boxed H?"

Stark stiffened at that question and the dying cowboy's feeble nod in response to it. If a Boxed H rider had been shot, that meant trouble out there, bad trouble.

"Set him down on the porch, careful-like," Brewster ordered the townies who still had hold of Charley Davenport's arms, keeping him up. They moved Charley over to the raised boardwalk and lowered him gently to the edge of it. He sat there, still hunched over with his arms crossed tightly over his bloody middle.

Brewster sat down beside him and put an arm around Charley's shoulders to hold him up. "I won't lie to you, son," he said quietly. "You're in a bad way. Can you tell me what happened out there?"

Charley nodded again, weakly. Stark knelt in front of him so that he could see the young cowboy's face as he answered. "It was Scott and . . . those gunslingers. The one called Cahoon . . . he shot me, claimed I was goin' for my gun, but I . . . I never . . ."

"Were you by yourself, Charley?" Stark asked.

A jerky shake of the head. "No. Mal and some of the boys . . . were there. We were lookin' for . . . for strays in the foothills."

"Out of the way, blast it," came the firm voice of Dr. Silcox as he pushed through the crowd. When he caught sight of Charley, he exclaimed, "Good Lord!"

Stark glanced up and said sharply, "Just a minute, Doc, and then you can tend to this youngster."

Brewster leaned his head closer to Charley's and asked, "Was there a gunfight between Cahoon's boys and the Boxed H crew?"

"Y-yeah," Charley gasped. "Guns goin' off everywhere. Mal and the other fellas . . . took off toward that old . . . old line shack. Don't know what happened . . . after that." He winced and clutched himself more tightly.

"Damn it, Sheriff, you're killing him," Silcox snapped. "I insist you let me see to him."

Brewster nodded and stood up. "Reckon we've heard enough." He raised his voice. "I'll be needin' a posse to ride with me out to the Hawthorne place."

There was no shortage of volunteers among the men who had heard Charley Davenport's story. No one took kindly to killers like Cahoon and his friends flaunting their presence in Delgado. Now the gunmen had gone too far with this attack on Malcolm Hawthorne and his ranch hands.

Stark was striding quickly toward the livery stable to fetch his Appaloosa when Todd Summers stepped out onto the porch of the mercantile with a frown on his face. "What's all the commotion about?"

Stark grimaced. All day he had been trying to get a moment alone with Summers, and now that he finally had it, he couldn't take advantage of it. Summers's indiscretions with Evelyn Rogers, whoever she was, paled to insignifance next to the murderous assault on Malcolm Hawthorne and his crew.

"A posse's riding to the Boxed H," he answered curtly. "Scott Hawthorne and Cahoon and those other gunmen are trying to kill Malcolm and some of the hands. They may have already done it for all I know."

Summers paled and said, "My God." He untied the long storekeeper's apron behind his back. "I'm going with you."

"You don't have to—"

"The hell I don't! This has gone on long enough. Scott and Malcolm are both my friends, and I won't stand by any longer while they destroy themselves!" Summers wadded up the apron and flung it aside. "Just let me get my gun and my horse."

"Be in front of the sheriff's office in five minutes, ready to ride," Stark told him, then headed on to the livery stable. Summers had surprised him with his vehemence. The merchant might have given in to the temptations of the flesh, as the sky pilots called it in their hellfire-and-brimstone sermons, but Summers seemed genuinely to care about the Hawthorne family.

What was left of it, anyway, Stark thought bleakly.

A few minutes later, with Brewster and Stark at its head, the posse thundered out of Delgado, heading west toward the Boxed H.

Malcolm leaned his head against the rough log wall behind him and closed his eyes. It had grown almost unbearably hot in the little cabin, and he was beginning to feel the effects of his wound.

Walt Parker had taken enough time away from the fight to tear some strips off the bottom of Malcolm's shirt and bind them tightly around his shoulder. That had eased the pain a little and slowed the bleeding. Malcolm felt light-headed, and over the past couple of hours the dull ache in his shoulder and arm had grown to a mass of throbbing agony. Damn Cahoon, he thought, and damn Scott, too.

"Not going to be much longer now," Parker said from where he was crouching by a loophole. "We'd have been out of ammunition before now if one of your boys hadn't thought to grab his saddlebags when he was jumping off his horse."

Parker had taken charge of the defense of the line shack like a military commander, ordering the two Boxed H hands to space their shots and make each one count rather than firing wildly at the trees as they had at first. That strategy had stretched their ammunition supply somewhat, and Parker had grunted in satisfaction when two of Cahoon's men were downed. That was all the damage the defenders had managed to inflict, but it was enough to keep the attackers at bay and keep them from charging the line shack.

Malcolm licked his dry lips and said hoarsely, "Maybe somebody will hear the shooting and come to help."

Parker shrugged without looking around. "Won't hurt to think so, I suppose," he said, "but I sure as hell wouldn't count on it."

Malcolm felt himself drifting toward unconsciousness and tightened his grip on the gun in his hand. He opened his eyes and shook his head. He wanted to be awake when the killers finally burst in. He wanted to be able to take at least one of them with him. It probably wouldn't be Cahoon—the big gunman would likely hang back a little and let the others come in first—and it definitely wouldn't be Scott. But at this point Malcolm would settle for what he could get.

The hammer of Parker's Lightning fell on an empty chamber. "That's it," he said. "No more for me."

"I'm out, too," one of the cowboys said.

"Same for me," added the other one.

An eerie silence settled over the interior of the cabin, punctuated by the gunshots still coming from outside. Malcolm braced his feet against the puncheon floor and pushed himself slowly up the wall at his back. He lifted the gun in his hand. "No need for you boys to die, too. I'm going out to meet them."

"You don't really think that'll do any good, do you?" Parker scoffed. "They'll kill us, too, after they've shot you to ribbons. Stay in here, you damned fool. Make 'em come to you."

Malcolm shook his head, ignoring a wave of dizziness. "I'm going out. I'll be on my feet when they come." He brandished the pistol weakly. "Don't try to stop me."

"Wouldn't think of it," Parker said in a tone as dry as caliche.

Malcolm dragged in a deep breath and took an unsteady step toward the door, then another and another. His left arm hung useless at his side. He used his right hand, the one holding the gun, to grasp the latch string. The shooting had stopped outside now, too, as if the killers were getting ready for their final charge.

"Don't do it, boss," said one of the Boxed H riders.

"My father would've died to defend this ranch," Malcolm said with a faint smile. "I can't do any less."

He yanked the door open, stumbled out into the brightness of the late afternoon sun, and lifted the revolver in his hand. The world seemed to explode in gunfire.

Stark, Brewster, and the other posse members had heard shooting long before they reached the battle scene. Brewster knew the approximate location of the line shack Charley Davenport had mentioned and was leading the riders toward it. The gunfire was a good sign, Stark thought; at least some of the Boxed H men must have reached the shack, forted up in it, and kept on fighting.

There was a lull in the firing as the posse swept up a ridge. The silence was an ominous one. Stark hoped it didn't mean the battle was over because one side had been wiped out. If that was the case, he knew which group had lost.

"Come on!" Brewster urged. "It ain't much farther now!"

The riders from Delgado topped the ridge and saw the little valley spread out before them. A faint haze hung over the scene, and Stark knew it was all the powder smoke floating in the air. A lot of gunpowder had been burned here this afternoon.

As the posse charged down the far side of the slope and across the valley, they passed the bodies of three men sprawled in unmistakable postures of death. Gunfire popped in the trees on the other side of the valley, and Stark saw fresh smoke drifting into the air. Bullets kicked up dirt in front of them.

"Cut loose, boys!" Brewster yelled. "Keep 'em hoppin'!"

The possemen spread out and opened fire. Stark slid his Winchester from its saddleboot and started throwing slugs into the trees as fast as he could work the lever. The Appaloosa ran steadily beneath him, guided by his knees. The big horse was used to the loud explosions and the stench of burned powder.

The posse numbered some twenty riders, and the odds must have been too much for Cahoon's men. They broke and ran, trying to reach their horses at the edge of the trees. Bullets cut them down, sending them sprawling on the ground. Stark saw Cahoon himself, his duster and his long pale hair both flapping, dashing toward the horses.

Stark jerked the Appaloosa to an abrupt halt to steady himself. He lined the sights of the Winchester on the racing figure, followed him expertly, and squeezed the trigger. The rifle cracked, and Cahoon spun off his feet, clutching a bullet-torn thigh as he fell and rolled over and over.

Urging the big horse to a run, Stark galloped up to Cahoon as the other members of the posse continued the cleanup. The killer had dropped his gun when he fell, and he was reaching for it when Stark pulled the Appaloosa to a stop. Stark jacked another shell into the rifle's chamber and said, "I wouldn't if I were you, Cahoon."

The gunslinger froze, then looked up at Stark, a snarl contorting his face. "You ain't me, you fat son of a bitch," he said, and his hand trembled over the gun. Slowly, though, he pulled it back. He sat up, stretched his bloody leg in front of him, and complained, "Look what you done to me."

"Less'n you deserve," Stark growled. He turned his head and saw the line shack through the trees. Malcolm Hawthorne was standing in front it, his left arm hanging limp by his side, his right hand grasping a revolver now pointed toward the ground. There was a look of astonishment on his face, as if he couldn't believe he was still alive. Behind him, Walt Parker and two Boxed H riders emerged from the shack, looking equally surprised. They were the only survivors from the Boxed H, Stark knew, because Charley Davenport had no doubt died by now back in Delgado.

Brewster and some of the other men from town were checking the fallen gunmen. The sheriff looked up from the grim task and called to Stark, "They're all dead. Looks like you corralled the only live one."

Stark nodded. At that moment someone rode up beside him and a voice called, "Watch out, Judge!" A pistol cracked wickedly.

Stark jerked around to see Todd Summers sitting on his horse, a smoking Colt in his hand. Cahoon was lying on his back now, a black-rimmed hole in his forehead where Summers's bullet had bored into his brain.

"What the hell!" Stark exploded. "Why'd you shoot him?"

Summers swung down from the saddle, stepped to the corpse of the gunman, and bent over him. When he straightened, he was holding a Prescott Paragon pocket revolver with a two-inch barrel. He held it out toward Stark and said, "The dirty sneak was about to use that belly gun on you, Judge. I saw him reaching for it as I rode up."

Stark grunted and took the gun. It was a .38 caliber, powerful enough to kill him if Cahoon had gotten off a shot.

"Guess I'm getting old," he said. "I thought all the fight had gone out of him." He looked at the storekeeper and nodded. "Thanks, Summers."

"I'm glad I was here, Judge."

Brewster came over to join them and looked down disdainfully at Cahoon's body. "Can't say as I'm sorry to see that one gone," he commented.

"Any sign of Scott Hawthorne?" asked Stark as he stuck the Prescott behind his belt. He was afraid the younger Hawthorne brother had been killed in the fighting.

However, Brewster jerked a thumb toward the trees and said, "He's over there, startin' to come around. When I said the rest of 'em was dead, I meant those gunfighters Cahoon brought in. Scott looks to be all right, 'cept for a lump on the side of his head."

Glad to hear that news, Stark dismounted and hurried over to where Scott Hawthorne was sitting against a tree trunk. His head hung between his upraised knees, and he was slowly shaking it from side to side.

Stark wasn't the only one converging on him. Malcolm was staggering toward him from the other direction. Raising the gun in his hand, he said shakily, "Killer! You murdering bastard!"

Stark lunged forward. His hand closed over the cylinder of the Colt and wrenched it out of Malcolm's grip. "Hold it!" he said. "It's over, Malcolm. No more killing."

"Malcolm . . . ?" Scott looked up at his brother, relief flooding his features. Malcolm was haggard and trembling, and bloody, makeshift bandages were tied around his left shoulder, but he was alive. Scott lifted a hand toward his brother. "God, Mal, I'm so sorry—"

"Scott, I'm goin' to have to put you under arrest," Sheriff Brewster said as he came up on Scott's other side. "You'll have to stand trial for your part in the killin' of those Boxed H hands."

Scott blinked in confusion. "But . . . but I didn't kill anybody, Sheriff. I never wanted anybody to get killed. I came out here to make peace with Malcolm."

"You don't make peace by bringing half a dozen gunslingers with you, Scott," Todd Summers put in as he strode over to join them. "Good Lord, what were you thinking?"

Scott looked at the hostile faces surrounding him and

shuddered. "I didn't mean for it to happen!" he wailed mournfully. "I didn't tell Cahoon to shoot Charley Davenport! He said Charley was going for his gun, but I don't think he was. I think Cahoon wanted to kill somebody! He was crazy, I tell you, crazy!"

Walt Parker moved up alongside Malcolm and said, "I know you folks don't have much use for me, but I can say this much if you'll listen. This kid's telling the truth about Cahoon. Davenport never tried to draw his gun. Cahoon shot him down in cold blood. After that—" Parker shrugged. "Well, after that there was no stopping it. I reckon that's what Cahoon wanted all along."

"It's true," Scott said hurriedly, pulling himself to his feet. "I tried to stop it. I told them to quit shooting, but they wouldn't do it. Cahoon said you were wounded, Mal, and I wanted to get help for you."

Malcolm's eyes were a little clearer now, and Stark wondered if he was in that twilight state on the edge of consciousness where the pain of a bullet wound receded somewhat. Sometimes that was a man's last chance to think clearly.

"Why should I believe you?" Malcolm asked his brother.

Scott wiped the back of his hand across his mouth. "Because it's the truth," he insisted. "No piece of land is worth brother trying to kill brother. I wish I'd never sent for Cahoon! I wish I'd ridden out and let you have the ranch." He took a deep breath. "Can you forgive me, Mal? Can you ever forgive me?"

For a long moment Malcolm didn't say anything. Then, slowly, he slid his gun back into its holster and put out his hand toward his brother. "I can try," he said in a hoarse whisper. "I can try if you can."

Scott clasped Malcolm's hand, and then the older brother was hugging the younger one, awkwardly because of his wounded arm. Stark watched the embrace and knew that the time had almost come for him to ride out of Delgado. A few details still remained to be worked out, but the war for the Boxed H was finally over.

Chapter Nineteen

Just as Stark had guessed, Charley Davenport died after the posse had left Delgado. Funeral services for him and the other four Boxed H cowboys killed in the fighting were held the next day. Cahoon and his fellow gunnies had already been laid to rest in Delgado's cemetery, without ceremony or mourners.

There had been too many funerals around here lately, Stark thought as he put on his hat and walked away from the cemetery when it was all over. First Emmitt Hawthorne's service—although there had been no body to bury—then Burton Garrison's, and now the five cowhands. Garrison's murder was still a mystery; Malcolm insisted that the will he had found was authentic and that he had had nothing to do with the lawyer's death. Walt Parker made the same claim, and Stark tended to believe him now.

"Could be it was that fella Cahoon causin' all the trouble," Brewster had speculated the night before, when he and Stark discussed the case in the sheriff's office. "He wanted to keep things stirred up 'tween Malcolm and Scott until there was a showdown and he could get away with killin' Malcolm. If Charley Davenport hadn't made it to town to fetch help, those Boxed H boys would've been wiped out, and Scott could've told any story he wanted about how it all happened. Reckon we would've always suspected things were wrong, but we wouldn't've been able to prove nothin'."

"Could be you're right," Stark had told him. "Maybe it was Cahoon. . . ."

But something still seemed loco about the whole thing, something he had maybe overlooked. In the light of day, though, Stark surely couldn't say what it was.

There was a stone wall about waist-high around the cemetery, and as Stark walked toward the arched, wrought-iron gate with the other mourners, he saw a scruffy figure leaning against the outside of the wall. Old Nat was wearing a solemn expression and a sling for his left arm. Stark turned toward him as he went through the gate.

"Looks like I missed the services," Nat said as Stark came up to him. "Should've got here earlier."

"What are you doing up and around?" asked Stark. "I figured you'd still be recuperating."

"Hell, I told you yesterday I ain't hurt bad, Judge. Took me a while to convince that sawbones, but he finally up and saw the error of his ways."

"You pestered him until he threw you out, isn't that what you mean?"

A grin split Nat's weathered face. "Somethin' like that. I hear all the trouble's over."

Stark nodded. "Seems to be. Sheriff Brewster decided not to press any charges against Scott, seeing as how he and Malcolm have decided to get along in the future. I talked to all three of the Hawthornes earlier today, and Malcolm's going to split the ranch up with his brother and sister. Scott's moving back out there, and he and Malcolm claim they're going to help each other run the ranch." Stark shook his head ruefully. "Wish they'd been that reasonable a week or so ago."

"What about Miss Lorna?"

"She'll get her share of the profits, even after she marries Todd Summers and moves into town."

Nat looked down at the ground and shuffled one booted foot back and forth. "What about that, ah, business with Summers and that other lady?"

"What about your blackmail scheme, you mean?" Stark shrugged. "I don't know if Summers hired those two hardcases to try to kill you or not. If he did, it didn't work. But I intend to have a talk with him anyway and set him straight. In fact, I think I'll do it right now." He had just spotted Todd Summers helping Lorna into a carriage with her brothers.

Stark turned away, and Nat called after him, "I'm sure sorry if I caused any trouble, Judge."

Stark waved a hand and went over to the storekeeper. "Could I have a word with you, Mr. Summers?"

Summers looked a little surprised, but he said, "Certainly, Judge. What about?"

A glance around told Stark that no one was standing within easy listening distance. Most of the people who had attended the graveside services were either riding away or walking back into town. He looked coldly at

Summers and said in a low, hard voice, "About a woman named Evelyn Rogers."

The man was a pretty good actor, Stark had to give him that. His eyes flickered a little and his jaw tightened slightly, but he controlled those reactions almost immediately. "Who?" he asked blandly.

Stark shook his head. "It's no use pretending, Summers. I know about you and the lady and your rendezvous with her at that old adobe cabin out by Blevins Hill. I know how that old prospector tried to blackmail you about it. And I've got a pretty good idea that you hired those two gunmen I killed to ambush him."

Summers grew paler with each word out of Stark's mouth. He said nervously, "I never . . . I swear I didn't mean to hurt anyone, not Lorna and not—"

"I don't give a damn what you meant to do, mister," Stark cut in, his eyes boring into Summers's. "I could stay here and make life hell for you up one way and down the other, but I don't have the time. I've got to head for El Paso tomorrow. So here's what you're going to do." His voice was still low enough that only he and Summers could hear it, but the menace in it was unmistakable. "You're going to tell this Evelyn Rogers you can't see her anymore, and it'd probably be a good idea if she was to leave town, too. Once you're married to Lorna Hawthorne, you're going to be faithful to her, and you're going to be the best damned husband any man ever was. You give her a lick of trouble, you hurt her in any way, and I'll be back here before you know it, coming down on you with both feet. I'm not sure why that gal even wants to marry you, but since she does, you're going to make it work. You understand that, you son of a bitch?"

Summers tried to call up a little righteous indignation. "I . . . I saved your life when Cahoon tried to kill you," he sputtered.

"And I thank you for it," Stark said. "But that won't stop me from making you regret it if you don't go along with what I just told you."

Summers stared at him for a moment longer. Then his eyes cut away in defeat. "All right. You don't really know how it is, but . . . all right. I understand, and I'll do as you say."

"Good. Remember that. And congratulations in advance on your wedding, since I likely won't be here for it."

Summers laughed humorlessly at that sally, and Stark turned to walk away. He wished Summers hadn't brought up that business with Cahoon. If the gunman really *was* about to pull that belly gun, then Summers had indeed saved his life.

Stark stopped abruptly, shook his head a little, and moved on with a frown on his face. His brain had tried to grasp something just then, but it was gone now.

Before another twenty-four hours had passed, he'd be gone from Delgado, too. But there was another errand he had to take care of first.

Jessica Prentice looked up from the desk and smiled as Stark came into the office. "Hello, Earl," she said softly. "I was hoping you'd stop by before you left."

"Won't be riding out until tomorrow." Stark sat down in the chair in front of her desk and perched his hat on his knee. "I thought maybe we could have dinner tonight."

A look of regret crossed Jessica's face. "I'm sorry. I wish we could. But I have so much work to do . . ."

She gestured at the pile of papers on the desk. "Some of this has to be finished by tomorrow."

Stark smiled slightly and shook his head. "The legal profession does have its drawbacks, doesn't it?" He reached forward and picked up some of the documents. "Maybe I could give you a hand so you could finish up quicker. I used to be a pretty fair prairie-dog lawyer, you know."

"Oh, no, that's not necessary." Jessica stood up quickly and came around the desk, taking the papers from him before he could do more than glance at them. She tossed them back onto the desk, then put her hands on Stark's shoulders as he stood up. "Sheriff Brewster tells me you used to be called Big Earl. Well, I'm going to miss you, Big Earl." She drew his face down to hers and kissed him.

After a long moment she pulled back, and Stark said quietly, "I'm going to miss you, too, Jessica. Maybe I'll get back this way someday. I intend to, but you never know, with my job and all."

"I understand," she whispered.

Stark squared his shoulders and put his mind back on business. "There's one more legal item that needs to be attended to. You've heard about Malcolm and Scott Hawthorne settling their differences?"

"Of course. Malcolm's going to give Scott and Lorna each a third of the ranch, isn't he?"

"That's right. It'd be a good idea if you were to draw up a formal agreement spelling all that out. That way, there won't be any question about it in the future."

"That's a good idea," Jessica agreed. "When they're ready, I'd be glad to—"

"Why don't you go ahead and draw it up?" Stark

suggested. "I'll be in town until tomorrow. We could ride out there together in the morning and let all three of them sign so I can witness it, and that'll give us a little more time together." He summoned up a smile. "Maybe we could even take a picnic with us."

"I thought you had to get to El Paso."

His broad shoulders lifted in a shrug. "I could put the trip off a couple of hours."

Jessica nodded. "Of course, Earl. I'll work on the document this afternoon, and we'll take it out to the Boxed H in the morning." She paused. "I hope Malcolm and Scott can continue getting along."

Stark frowned. "You reckon they won't?"

"Oh, I hope they do, of course. But there was so much bad blood between them . . . well, I hope they don't have another falling-out before we can get that document signed."

"I don't think that'll happen," Stark said. "I saw those boys, and I think they're genuinely sorry for everything that happened. I reckon if old Emmitt Hawthorne could see 'em and know how it all wound up, he'd be proud of them."

"Well, it's nice to think so, anyway," Jessica said. "Now, you'd better get going, Earl. I have even more work to do now that I have to draw up that agreement."

"Sure." Stark smiled at her, turned, and left the office. As he stepped outside, the cheerful mask fell, leaving his bearded face bleak. The last few minutes had cost him quite an effort—the wheels of his brain were revolving madly, and he didn't want Jessica troubled by the thoughts going through his head. As he walked down the street, he remembered all the things he had seen and heard since coming to Delgado, recalled something he himself had said that had been the key to unlock the final door. It all made sense now, at least a sort of sense. To use one of his pa's expressions, Stark had all his ducks in a row.

And there was nothing stupider than a duck, Stark mused, unless it was a judge who just didn't want to see the truth until it was damned near too late.

He stepped up his pace. He had to have a long talk with Sheriff Brewster.

Chapter Twenty

It was mighty good to be back home, Scott Hawthorne thought that night as he walked down a hallway in the big, rambling ranch house. The Boxed H had never looked so good to him. An air of mourning hung over the place, but it was tempered by a feeling that the future would be better. Some of the hands were a little hostile toward him because of his part in bringing Cahoon and the other gunslingers to Delgado, but he was hopeful that would wear off once they saw how determined he was to make up for his past mistakes. That afternoon, after returning from the funerals in town, he and Malcolm and Lorna had ridden out on the range together, as they had when they were kids, and he was sure they could get back what they had once had between them.

If only they got the chance.

In the meantime, things were quiet on the ranch tonight. Lorna had already turned in, and Malcolm was in the study working, trying to make sense of the Boxed H's finances. Scott had offered to help him with the work—after all, he knew more about that part of the ranch's operation than Malcolm did—but Malcolm had insisted on muddling through it by himself. He seemed to think he would learn more that way.

Well, Scott thought, Mal would accept his help in time.

He stepped into his father's library. Emmitt Hawthorne had been a well-read man, and during his youth Scott had read many of the volumes in this room. In the past few years he had gotten away from that, preferring to spend his time drinking and gambling and having a good time with the girls who worked at the Red Horse and the other saloons in town. Maybe it was time he reversed that. Shoot, it was past time. He would find something in here he hadn't read, maybe start improving his mind again.

He heard a faint step behind him, a rustle of cloth, and then a heavy object slammed into the back of his head. Scott pitched forward, out cold, his face skidding on the rug. A figure bent over him, checked quickly to make sure he was still breathing, then crossed the room to blow out the lamp on the reading table. The attacker returned to where Scott lay, stooped, grasped him under the arms, and lifted him with a grunt. Careful not to make too much noise, he dragged Scott out of the library and started down the hall toward the study where Malcolm Hawthorne was struggling with ranch paperwork.

The hall was dark and shadowy, illuminated only by

the slice of lamplight coming through the partially open door of the study. The intruder stopped just outside the door and lowered Scott's senseless form to the floor, moving quietly so as not to alert Malcolm, who seemed engrossed by the figures written in the ledger in front of him on Emmitt Hawthorne's old rolltop desk. Like a living shadow, the intruder slipped through the doorway and glided noiselessly toward Malcolm. A hand lifted, the fingers wrapped around the hilt of a knife. Lamplight gleamed on the blade as it paused at the top of its arc, ready to be driven down into Malcolm's back.

Judge Earl Stark stepped out from behind the open door, jammed the barrel of his pistol against the intruder's spine, and grated, "Drop that knife, Summers, or this LeMat'll blow you plumb in half."

Todd Summers turned as stiff as a statue of Confederate soldiers on a courthouse lawn. Stark reached up with his free hand and plucked the knife from his unresisting fingers.

Meanwhile, Malcolm turned around, a look of anger and disappointment on his face. "I didn't believe the judge at first, Todd. Hell, you were going to be my brother-in-law. I didn't want to think you were a killer."

Summers looked pale and stricken, even more so than when Stark had confronted him earlier in the day about Evelyn Rogers. He opened his mouth a couple of times without saying anything, then finally managed to get some words out. "It-it's not what it looks like, Mal. I wouldn't—"

"Save it," Malcolm snapped coldly. "Where's my brother?"

"Look out in the hall," Stark advised him. "He had

to have Scott close by so that he could leave him to take the blame after he killed you."

Malcolm stood up and hurried past Stark and Summers, calling from the hallway, "He's out here, all right! Looks like Summers hit him on the head and knocked him out."

While Malcolm tended to his brother, Stark said to his prisoner, "What were you going to do, Summers? Pretend to stumble on the scene right after Scott had knifed Malcolm in the back? After everything that's happened, a jury would've likely believed that, and Scott would've been hanged for murder. With Malcolm dead, too, that would leave the Boxed H completely to Lorna, and to you once you'd married her."

"That's insane," croaked Summers.

"Damn right it is, but you helped cook it up. Reckon about six months or so after the wedding, Lorna would've had some sort of accident. As far as anybody knows, she's the last of the Hawthornes, so the Boxed H would go to you." Stark jabbed the LeMat a little harder into Summers's back. "Turn around."

Shakily, Summers turned to face Stark. "I don't care if you are a judge, you can't get away with railroading me—"

"I'm not getting away with anything. You put the rope right around your own neck tonight, Summers."

Malcolm helped a moaning Scott into the room and lowered him into the chair in front of the desk. Scott lifted a hand to the knot on his head and said, "Sorry, Judge. I shouldn't have let him knock me out that way. Almost ruined the whole trap."

"Well, not really," Stark said. "We stopped him in time to save you and Mal and your sister, and that's what counts. Too bad we couldn't have saved Burton Garrison, too, but he had to die once he'd figured out the truth about that so-called will."

"Then it *is* a fake?" Malcolm asked.

Stark nodded. "Yep, and a damned good one."

Scott stopped massaging the bump on his head long enough to ask, "If the will's a forgery, why didn't it have everything left to Lorna to start with?"

"That would have been even more suspicious than having one of you boys inherit the whole shooting match," Stark replied. "Besides, you'd have still been around to cause trouble for him if anything happened to Lorna after the wedding. This way, all three of you would eventually be out of the way."

"A forgery," Malcolm mused. "It's hard to believe."

"Summers had plenty of chances to plant it, since he was out here all the time visiting Lorna. He may have even planted the idea in her head for Malcolm to take one last look around before the hearing. Anyway, the will served its purpose, which was to keep things stirred up between you two hotheads. Same thing for all those bushwhack attempts. It was Cahoon's job to make sure you two hated each other so much that when one of you wound up dead, the other one would naturally be convicted of the murder."

Scott stared at Summers. "Cahoon was really working for him?"

"Maybe not at first, but Summers recruited him fast enough. That's why Summers had to kill him when we captured him after that gunfight at the line shack. He didn't want Cahoon spilling the story. So he shot Cahoon and planted that belly gun on him to make everybody think he'd saved my life. Mighty slick work, Summers."

"You don't have any proof of that," Summers insisted nervously. "You can't prove anything except that I came into this room with a knife in my hand. You don't know what I intended to do with it." Some of his self-confidence was seeping back. "Think about it. I'm no forger. I didn't write that will, and that's what caused all the trouble between Malcolm and Scott. Without that, you would have just divided the ranch equally among them and Lorna."

"True enough." The gun in Stark's hand didn't waver as he covered Summers. "Your partner Evelyn Rogers forged the will. She's got a real knack for copying the way other folks write. I'll bet if we did some checking, we'd find that she did some jail time for forgery in the past." He sighed. "Well, we'll take you on back to town and arrest her, too."

"You won't have to go back to Delgado to find me, Earl," Jessica Prentice said as she stepped into the room behind Stark. "And that was a good guess about the jail time. Unfortunately, you're right. But I don't intend to go back to jail, ever again."

Stark's pulse hammered in his head. He could tell by Jessica's tone that she was armed, and when he glanced over his shoulder, he saw the little pistol she was pointing at him. It was another Prescott Paragon, but it seemed to be a larger caliber than the one Summers had planted on Cahoon. At this range it would blow a good-sized hole in his back if she squeezed the trigger.

Malcolm and Scott both looked stunned. Stark hadn't explained all of his theory to them when he was setting up the trap for Summers, only the basic facts about the storekeeper's involvement. Both brothers stayed where they were. Jessica could swing the gun to cover them in a split second, and the Prescott held five shots, enough for all of them.

Without lowering the LeMat, Stark said quietly, "Hello, Jessica. Or should I call you Evelyn?"

"I prefer Jessica, actually. I've gone to a great deal of trouble to bury Evelyn Rogers. Forging my legal credentials wasn't the easiest job I've ever done, you know."

"Why'd you use your real name to pay the back taxes on that house?" Stark asked.

Jessica laughed. "I didn't want anyone to connect me with it once I started meeting Todd there. The whole matter was handled through the mail so that no one could identify me. It was a bit unusual, but I knew Edward Sprague wasn't smart enough to suspect anything. Besides, he was so glad to have the back taxes cleared up he didn't bother to look into things."

Malcolm spoke up. "I don't believe this. How long have the two of you been . . . been . . ."

"Lovers?" Jessica finished for him. "I didn't know Todd when I came to Delgado. I was looking for a place to lie low for a while and scout around for something that would pay off big. We got together pretty soon after I arrived. We're two of a kind, I suppose you could say, and when Emmitt Hawthorne died without a will, we knew the time had come to make our move."

"That's enough talking," Summers growled. "Hand over that gun, Judge. Your little plan didn't work."

Stark hesitated, then turned the LeMat butt-first and gave it to Summers. "Would've worked," he said disgustedly. "I didn't expect to see Jessica out here tonight."

She said, "You didn't really think that hick sheriff

could keep an eye on me and stop me from slipping out of town, did you, Earl? How much did you tell him about me?"

"Not enough, I reckon." Stark grunted. "I didn't want to lay it all out for Brewster until I had some proof. I've got it now."

Summers laughed harshly. "Too late to do you any good."

Now that he was disarmed, Stark turned slowly to face Jessica. He wanted to keep her talking, wanted to clear up a few last details. "How did Garrison figure out the will was a fake?" he asked. "Did he stumble on to your skills as a forger and put it together from that, like I did?"

Jessica frowned at the reminder of her law partner's death. "I have a bad habit," she said. "When I'm concentrating, I scribble on a pad of paper—in other people's handwriting. I was afraid you had noticed that this afternoon, especially after you suggested I draw up that agreement for the Hawthornes. Todd and I were afraid you might be up to something; that's why I followed him out here tonight. But in case you weren't, we had to go ahead and get one of the brothers out of the way so the other one could be framed for the murder."

Stark jerked his head toward the storekeeper. "So Summers killed Garrison, and he was on his way to your house to tell you that everything was all right when Brewster and I showed up and ran him off, thinking that you were in danger from him, too."

"I wish I'd killed *you* that night, too," Summers said bitterly. "There would have been a lot less trouble."

"And those two gunnies you hired after Nat tried to

blackmail you—were they supposed to kill both of us?"

Summers shrugged. "It would have been all right if they had. You're the luckiest son of a bitch I've ever seen, Stark. But your luck's run out now." He lifted the LeMat a little.

"It won't work now. You've lost your chance," Stark told them.

"It *will* work," insisted Jessica, "when Sheriff Brewster comes out here and discovers that Scott and Malcolm went mad and shot it out with each other. Poor Lorna will be devastated, and Todd will be right there to comfort her and marry her and inherit the whole ranch when she dies later."

"What about me?" Stark asked, knowing he wouldn't like the answer.

"You and I will be long gone before the tragedy takes place," Jessica replied.

"And I'll dispose of your body later," Summers added, sounding almost gleeful at the prospect. "If we're lucky, folks will think you left town once your legal chores were over."

"Luck has nothing to do with it," Jessica said. "People know that Earl and I were friends. If I say he told me good-bye before he left, no one will have any reason to doubt the story."

Stark looked at her and said, "I thought for a while there we really were friends, Jessica."

She smiled at him, her blue eyes chunks of ice. "I think you're the most dangerous one, Earl. I'll be glad when you're dead. Now move, so Todd can get started with his part of the job."

Summers took a small pistol from his pocket and

tucked the LeMat behind his belt. He smiled at Malcolm and Scott.

Stark stayed where he was. He shook his head and said to Jessica, "Nope. You're going to have to shoot me right here. That'll play hob with your little plan, won't it?"

Her jaw tensed. "Don't argue with me, Earl. I'll kill you now if I have to. I'll have to make up some other story people will believe. I'm good at it, you know."

Stark didn't budge, and Jessica's lips drew back in a grimace. The barrel of her Prescott came up a little more, her finger tightening on the trigger.

That was when a figure came leaping through the door from the darkened hallway and slammed into Jessica from behind, driving her to the floor and knocking the gun from her hand. It spun along the floor toward Stark.

Summers was already pivoting toward the judge, a curse on his lips. Stark threw himself down as Summers's gun blasted. The slug whipped over his head. His fingers slapped the butt of the spinning gun, closed around it, brought the weapon up, and cocked it as he angled the barrel toward Summers. Stark was lying on his side as he fired. The .41 caliber slug ripped into the storekeeper's belly and drove him backward. Stark fired twice more, just to make sure.

Meanwhile, Jessica had twisted around in the grip of the old man struggling with her and slammed her clubbed fists across his bearded features. The old desert rat known as Nat fell away from her, his grip loosening. She lunged to her feet and bolted through the door before anyone could stop her.

Stark scrambled to his feet, knelt beside the fallen Summers long enough to make sure he was dead, then swung around to face Nat. "Thought for a minute you weren't going to get here in time, Hawthorne. I'm glad I had you keeping an eye on Jessica."

"Hawthorne!" Malcolm and Scott exclaimed.

The old prospector was puffing and wheezing, trying to catch his breath after the struggle. "That gal . . . couldn't give me the slip . . . as easy as she did that star-packer!"

Stark headed for the door, pausing to put a hand on Nat's shoulder. "Was she on horseback?"

The old-timer nodded. "Horse was tied around back. You goin' after her?"

Before Stark could answer, a frightened Lorna, wearing a long white nightgown, appeared in the doorway. "I heard a gun—" She clapped her hands to her mouth and screamed when she saw the body of Todd Summers sprawled on the other side of the room.

"Damn right I'm going after her," Stark said to Nat. "You stay here and keep an eye on things. And you've got a lot of explaining to do to these youngsters."

Nat nodded solemnly. Malcolm and Scott both had their arms around Lorna, holding her back from Summers's body and telling her what had happened.

Stark pounded out of the house and headed toward the barn where he had hidden the Appaloosa earlier in the evening. Some of the Boxed H hands were running from the bunkhouse, anxious to see what all the commotion was about. Stark waved them on toward the ranch house when they asked him if he needed any help.

This was one chore he intended to take care of himself.

Moments later he was mounted and galloping down

the road toward Delgado. Knowing what he knew now about Jessica, he was fairly certain she would have some money stashed back in town to use for a quick getaway if she ever needed it. She needed it now, Stark figured.

The Appaloosa's long, powerful stride ate up the ground. Even carrying a man as big as Stark, the horse was fast. But Jessica's mount was a good one, too. She was a skilled rider, he recalled, and she had several minutes' lead on him.

It didn't matter, Stark told himself. One way or another, he was going to catch her.

The moon was nearly full, and it cast a brilliant silver light over the west Texas landscape. Stark spotted Jessica as he topped a ridge. The long slope on the other side led down into the valley of the Espantosa River. She was several hundred yards ahead of him, nearing the bridge over the gorge.

The bridge, Stark thought, his eyes widening. Even though it was fairly safe to cross now, the repairs were not yet complete. Only a short portion of the railing along the south side had been replaced. If Jessica's horse took a misstep . . .

He urged the Appaloosa on to greater speed.

He was close enough to hear the thud of her horse's hooves on the planks of the bridge, close enough to hear the shrill whinny of fear from the animal as it lost its balance and started to fall. Jessica had time to scream once as she sailed out of the saddle. The horse tumbled over once, caught itself, came to its feet, and then picked its way carefully across the remaining length of the span. The Espantosa bridge had never been meant for a horse careening along out of its rider's control.

Stark reined in. There was no sign of Jessica on the bridge.

Despite what he had learned about her, he felt hollow in the pit of his stomach as he heeled the Appaloosa to a walk. No need to hurry now. When he reached the bridge, he rode slowly across and back, leaning over to look at the trusses below to make sure Jessica hadn't managed to grab on to one of them. She was gone, though, no doubt about it.

He pointed the Appaloosa back toward the Boxed H. If things had only been different . . .

But things were never different. They were only the way they were, and Stark had known that for a long time.

Nat was waiting on the porch when Stark rode up to the ranch house. "You catch up with her?" he asked as Stark swung down from the Appaloosa.

"Nope. But the Espantosa Gorge did."

"Good Lord. You don't mean . . . ?"

Stark nodded grimly.

"Well," Nat mused, "some might say it was fittin', seein' as how all this got started. You must think me and Emmitt are a couple of sorry old men."

"Where is he now?" Stark asked. "You never did tell me the whole story."

"Waitin' on my hacienda, south o' the border a good ways." Nat sat down on the porch steps. "Yep, I started the place a long time ago, 'bout the same time Emmitt was startin' the Boxed H. When I never came back, I reckon most folks thought I was dead. But Emmitt and me, we got word to each other ever' now and then, so's we'd know the other one was still kickin'. I never figured he'd show up on my doorstep one day, though.

218

Hadn't seen the old codger in over thirty years, since before he brought Lila out here and those youngsters were born. Mal and Scott and Lorna never knew their ol' Uncle Nat."

"Did Emmitt plan that accident to make it look like he was dead?"

Nat shook his head. "Nope. It really was an accident, pure and simple. Emmitt had got out of the carriage to lead the horse across the bridge 'cause it was sort of skittish on account of the high water, which was roarin' somethin' awful that day. He felt somethin' hit the bridge, most likely a log that floated down from the mountains, and felt it startin' to go. The horse bolted for the far side and didn't make it. Emmitt let go and managed to get back off the way he'd come. But when he saw the horse and the carriage go off into the gorge, he knew if he didn't show up in town or at the ranch, folks'd probably think he was dead."

"So he took advantage of the opportunity to see what his children would do in that case."

"Yep, that was about it, all right. He figured Mal and Scott'd go to fightin' like a pack of wolves if they thought he was dead. But he wanted to know for sure. So he lit out for the border, walkin' part of the way and then ridin' a horse he bought from some poor farmer down close to the Rio. When he got to my place, he told me what he'd done and asked me if I'd come up and sort of keep an eye on the young uns for him and let him know what happened."

Stark squinted at the old man. "So you're not really a prospector who's never struck it rich?"

"Hell, no! I found a vein of silver the first year and used it to start a ranch. You can ride for a week down there in Chihuahua and still be on my hacienda. I'm a big skookum he-wolf down yonder. They call me Don Nataniel."

Stark lifted his eyebrows. "Nathaniel Hawthorne?"

Nat shrugged and said, "Don't reckon my folks'd ever heard of that writin' feller when they named me. And I ain't never got confused with him, specially not in Mexico."

Stark was too tired to laugh. Instead, he asked, "How are the kids?"

"They're shook up some, specially Lorna, but I reckon they'll be all right. Emmitt never really trusted that Summers feller, even though Lorna had her daddy wrapped around her little finger so tight he didn't have no choice but to give his blessin' to their engagement. That's why I was pokin' around Summers's business and found out about that woman of his. Wanted to see what he'd do when I goosed him a little about it." Nat shook his head. "I don't reckon even Emmitt had any idea what kind of low-down skunk Summers really was."

"What are you going to do now?"

Nat rubbed his bearded jaw. "Well, I found out what Emmitt wanted to know. Mal and Scott settled down and finally figured out they'd be better off workin' together. Reckon I'll send word to Emmitt down in Mexico right away to let him know that he can come back. Might stick around awhile myself."

"Good," Stark said. "It may take both of you to deal with how folks are going to feel now that they know the two of you have been playing games with them. Those youngsters may not like it much once they've had a chance to think about it."

Nat grimaced and looked uneasy. "Yeah, maybe we

didn't really think about what we was doin' long enough...."

Stark shook his head, stepped off the porch, and swung up onto the Appaloosa. He touched a finger to the brim of his hat. "Good luck to you and your brother, Nat. I have a feeling you're going to need it."

He turned the horse and rode away. He was ready to put this part of the country behind him, after he had stopped in Delgado and filled Sheriff Brewster in on everything that had happened. He'd had enough of greed and deception for a while. Things were seldom ever what they seemed, he thought, a faint smile tugging at his mouth. Look at him—he was a judge, of all things.

But inside he was still the man called Big Earl.

Epilogue

"... *And so, young gentlemen, you see that the things in which you believe may sometimes be only an example of the grossest mendacity, perpetrated by the most devious of prevaricators. Believe little of what you hear, my friends, and not even all of what you see. Because the most attractive of façades may conceal a veritable tapestry of deceit! A compendium of lies! Or, as we put it in those not-so-long-ago days, a whole passel of bull droppings!*

"I see that some of you look rather alarmed at the prospect, as if you fear that you are being sent from these halls of learning into a world full of bald-faced liars, where nothing and no one can be trusted. I assure you, that is not the case. Be cautious, yes. Ask questions, and when in doubt ... ask some more questions. But know, gentlemen, there are always some things on which you can depend.

"Number one, a good horse. Number two, a good dog. Number three—and don't try to make anything of the order in which I'm giving these to you, boys. Don't forget I was a lawyer, too. I'm making it up as I go along. And number three, a woman who laughs in your face only occasionally. And, of course, myself, your distinguished commencement speaker. You can believe everything *I* tell you.

"Well, that's all I've got to say. Go out there and practice law and try not to get in too much trouble. Now, is there a place around here where a man can get a drink? This public speaking is mighty thirsty work...."

**STARK'S JUSTICE: VOLUME THREE
THE DIABLO GRANT**
by James M. Reasoner

The Diablo Valley is some of the finest ranch land in New Mexico Territory, homesteaded over the years by courageous, hardworking men like Travis Richmond and Ben Tompkins. But the peaceful life they've created for themselves and their children is shattered when someone discovers an old Spanish document that deeds the entire valley to the Espina family and its heirs.

Is the document authentic? If it is, will the law uphold the granting of this productive, valuable land to old Juan Espina, the sole remaining member of the family, who is also the town drunk? Judge Earl Stark is brought in to decide the case.

Stark knows he is tangling with emotional as well as legal issues, and his task becomes more difficult when Juan Espina is murdered. The battle over Diablo Valley moves from Stark's makeshift courtroom to the valley itself as the ranchers who have tamed the land fight to hold on to what they believe is theirs—no matter what the law says.

Read THE DIABLO GRANT, on sale January 1995 wherever Pocket Books are sold.

About the Author

Judge Earl Stark is the latest creation of veteran author James Reasoner, who has written over seventy novels, including westerns, mysteries, and historical sagas. A lifelong Texan and a member of the Western Writers of America, Reasoner has worked as a newspaper columnist and bookstore manager in addition to his fiction writing. He is an avid reader and tries to write the sort of books he enjoys reading. Reasoner and his wife Livia (who also writes novels, under the name L.J. Washburn) live in the Texas countryside with their two daughters, Shayna and Joanna, and an assortment of dogs, cats, ducks, and Nigerian dwarf goats. He hopes to someday have a better fence.

Now a Major Motion Picture
from Columbia Pictures
Starring Jason Patric, Robert Duvall,
Gene Hackman, and Wes Studi as...

GERONIMO
— AN AMERICAN LEGEND —

**IN A LAND OF WARRIORS,
IN A TIME OF LEGENDS,
HE WAS THE GREATEST OF ALL.**
His Name Would Never Be Forgotten.

A Novel by Robert J. Conley
Based on a Story by John Milius
Screenplay by John Milius and Larry Cross

Available from Pocket Books

The *only* authorized biography of the legendary man who inspired two of the year's biggest movie events!

WYATT ☆ EARP
FRONTIER MARSHAL

"No man could have a more loyal friend than Wyatt Earp might be, nor a more dangerous enemy."
— Bat Masterson

"Earp never hunted trouble, but he was ready for any that came his way." —Jimmy Cairns, deputy marshal, Wichita, Kansas

"I am not ashamed of anything I ever did." — Wyatt Earp

Available in paperback from Pocket Books
mid-June 1994

THE BEST WESTERN NOVELS COME FROM POCKET BOOKS

Sam Brown
- ☐ THE CRIME OF COY BELL.............78543-5/$3.99
- ☐ THE BIG LONELY..........86547-1/$3.99

Robert J. Conley
- ☐ GO-AHEAD RIDER.......74365-1/$3.50
- ☐ BORDER LINE............74931-5/$3.99
- ☐ TO MAKE A KILLING....77900-1/$3.99
- ☐ NED CHRISTIE'S WAR....75969-8/$3.99
- ☐ GERONIMO: AN AMERICAN LEGEND....88982-6/$5.50
- ☐ ZEKE PROCTOR: CHEROKEE OUTLAW: ...77901-X/$4.99

D.R. Bensen
THE TRACKER
- ☐ #6: DEATHWIND............73839-9/$3.50

Jack Curtis
- ☐ CUT AND BRANDED.....79321-7/$3.99
- ☐ WILD RIVER MASSACRE.......79320-9/$3.99
- ☐ THE MARK OF CAIN......79316-0/$3.99

James M. Reasoner
- ☐ STARK'S JUSTICE..........87140-4/$3.99
- ☐ THE HAWTHORNE LEGACY ....87141-2/$4.99

Dusty Richards
- ☐ FROM HELL TO BREAKFAST ....87241-9/$3.99

R.C. House
- ☐ TRACKDOWN AT IMMIGRANT LAKE........76042-4/$3.50
- ☐ REQUIEM FOR A RUSTLER....................76043-2/$3.99
- ☐ RYERSON'S MANHUNT................87243-5/$3.99

Jim Miller
THE EX-RANGERS
- ☐ #9: CARSTON'S LAW......74827-0/$3.50
- ☐ #10: STRANGER FROM NOWHERE.................74828-9/$3.99
- ☐ #11: SOUTH OF THE BORDER................74829-7/$3.99

Giles Tippette
- ☐ THE BUTTON HORSE....79347-0/$4.50
- ☐ THE HORSE THIEVES....79345-4/$3.99
- ☐ SLICK MONEY...............79346-2/$4.50

Bruce H. Thorstad
- ☐ THE TIMES OF WICHITA ....70657-8/$3.50
- ☐ THE GENTS ....75904-3/$3.99
- ☐ PALO DURO................75905-1/$3.99
- ☐ SHARPSHOOTERS.........75906-X/$3.99
- ☐ ACE OF DIAMONDS........88583-9/$3.99

Simon & Schuster Mail Order
200 Old Tappan Rd., Old Tappan, N.J. 07675

Please send me the books I have checked above. I am enclosing $_____ (please add $0.75 to cover the postage and handling for each order. Please add appropriate sales tax). Send check or money order—no cash or C.O.D.'s please. Allow up to six weeks for delivery. For purchase over $10.00 you may use VISA: card number, expiration date and customer signature must be included.

Name _____
Address _____
City _____ State/Zip _____
VISA Card # _____ Exp.Date _____
Signature _____ 728-04